SPECIAL M[ ]**RS**

THE ULVERS[ ]**ON**
(registered UK[ ]373)

was established in 1972 to provide funds for research, diagnosis and treatment of eye diseases. Examples of major projects funded by the Ulverscroft Foundation are:-

- The Children's Eye Unit at Moorfields Eye Hospital, London
- The Ulverscroft Children's Eye Unit at Great Ormond Street Hospital for Sick Children
- Funding research into eye diseases and treatment at the Department of Ophthalmology, University of Leicester
- The Ulverscroft Vision Research Group, Institute of Child Health
- Twin operating theatres at the Western Ophthalmic Hospital, London
- The Chair of Ophthalmology at the Royal Australian College of Ophthalmologists

You can help further the work of the Foundation by making a donation or leaving a legacy. Every contribution is gratefully received. If you would like to help support the Foundation or require further information, please contact:

THE ULVERSCROFT FOUNDATION
The Green, Bradgate Road, Anstey
Leicester LE7 7FU, England
Tel: (0116) 236 4325

website: www.foundation.ulverscroft.com

30130504768155

Panos Karnezis was born in Greece in 1967 and moved to England in 1992. He studied engineering and worked in industry, then was awarded an MA in Creative Writing by the University of East Anglia. His work has been shortlisted for awards, broadcast on BBC Radio 4, and appeared in *Granta*, *New Writing 11*, *Prospect* and *Areté*. He lives in London.

THE FUGITIVES

In a remote corner of a Latin American rainforest, Father Thomas, a Catholic priest, comes across a badly wounded soldier and takes him to his church in an Indian village. The Indians, whose traditional way of life is under threat from outsiders, are wary of this new arrival. Venustiano, the proud young head of the community, is determined to protect his people, but feels powerless against the forces around him — and trusts nobody, not even Father Thomas. Meanwhile, a bloodthirsty jaguar prowls the area. As the only Indian with a gun, Venustiano means to use it . . .

Books by Panos Karnezis
Published by Ulverscroft:

THE CONVENT

PANOS KARNEZIS

◆

THE FUGITIVES

Complete and Unabridged

ULVERSCROFT
Leicester

First published in Great Britain in 2016 by
Vintage
London

First Large Print Edition
published 2017
by arrangement with
Vintage
Penguin Random House
London

A catalogue record for this book is available
from the British Library.

ISBN 978–1–4448–3335–5

Published by
F. A. Thorpe (Publishing)
Anstey, Leicestershire

Set by Words & Graphics Ltd.
Anstey, Leicestershire
Printed and bound in Great Britain by
T. J. International Ltd., Padstow, Cornwall

For, after all, what is man in nature? A nothing compared to the infinite, a whole compared to the nothing, a middle point between all and nothing, infinitely remote from an understanding of the extremes.

Blaise Pascal

Part One

1

The mud cushioned his fall and he stayed face-down where he fell, hoping that they had missed him in the pale evening light and the warm heavy rain. The machine gun that had killed his driver and wounded him had turned silent, but the fighting continued farther back, where the rest of the convoy had come to a halt. He heard the cannon of the Panhard desperately returning fire — then an explosion silenced it. The exchange of fire continued, but he rose to his feet and ran, expecting the machine gun to open up on him again, but the man in charge of it had probably gone to join the attack on the rest of the convoy.

He plodded through the mud towards the trees where the ground was firmer, and kept going deeper into the forest, away from the firefight. The pain in his arm seeped into his flesh, giving him a burning sensation. He had no idea which direction to go: his only thought was to get as far away from the ambush as he could. The sun had not set yet, but the canopy of the trees blocked most of the light, obscuring his way, and he stumbled and fell again and again. Sometimes he landed on his wounded arm and screamed, burying his face in the dirt to muffle the sound. When, finally, he paused to get his breath back, he noticed that the shooting had stopped: now they would come after him. He was shivering. The rain still fell heavily and his shirt was drenched and covered in mud. He did not take it off. It was his only protection against the sharp bushes and the mosquitoes. He went on, trying not to think about the seriousness of his wound; he had an idea that it hurt less that way.

The silence followed him. Whenever he stopped and listened, he heard only the tapping of the rain: they had not come after him. He went on with the moon shining palely through the trees now, lighting his way through the forest. At a stream he stopped at last. He thought: I am saved — then a stab of pain in his wounded arm made him lose his conviction. He took off his shirt and wrung it out. His wound was still bleeding, so he pulled off his belt and tied it round his arm. He still had some tablets for his altitude sickness and took two, but they had as little effect on the pain as on his constant shortness of breath. He could not carry on, it was very dark now, and so he sat underneath a tall mahogany where the earth was dry to wait for daylight. Soon he stopped taking any notice of the noises of the forest and drifted off while watching the rain. In his sleep he heard a young woman laughing somewhere in the forest. The voice sounded nearby, but he could not find her — when he got to the place that he thought she was, the voice seemed to come from somewhere else. He called, 'Hello, hello?' but there was no reply, only laughter. And the rain kept falling heavily . . .

When he opened his eyes it was well past daybreak: he had overslept. He sat staring at the sun, which shone through the tree branches, then something brushed against the undergrowth some twenty yards away. A spotted yellow skin showed for a moment through the grass and disappeared again. He knew what it was, even though he had never seen a jaguar before. He tried to think how to defend himself: he had dropped his pistol when he had jumped off the jeep. There were no stones within reach, just a few sticks, which would be of no use against a jaguar. He felt despair — to have survived the ambush, but then to be killed by an animal. A few seconds passed while he waited, curled up with his back against the tree. The jaguar appeared again through the undergrowth. The man's heart pounded in his breast and his eyes stayed fixed on the animal with an appalled expression. It did not come any closer. It moved leisurely away from him, back into the forest. He stayed where he was for a while: the jaguar could be nearby and he did not want to do anything that might provoke it. When he resumed his journey, he took the opposite direction from the one in which the animal had gone. He could not orientate himself, but even if he had had a compass it would have been of no use, since he had no idea which way he needed to go.

It did not rain that morning and he made what he thought was good progress. His arm had gone numb while he slept. It still hurt, but the suffering of the previous day had eased enough to allow him a little hope. At midday, with the sun beaming down, he came to a river at a place where the waters seemed shallow. The current was strong, but it seemed to him that the forest was less dense on the other side, and he decided to get across. When he took his boots off, he thought he heard something from the direction of the trees. He presumed it was the jaguar again, and quickly put his boots back on, picked up a heavy stick and backed into the water like some prehistoric man prepared to defend himself: human life could revert to its primal state in a flash. His earlier fear had returned, mixed with indignation, as if the animal were playing a cruel game on him. The blood rushed to his head, and he planted his feet into the muddy riverbed, prepared to stand his ground.

A man pulling a mule casually walked out of the forest. He did not seem threatening, just curious, and he had a fair complexion — a foreigner. The lieutenant came out of the water. 'Do you live round here?' he said without hope. The mule was packed and covered in mud: the stranger was on a long journey. 'I'm trying to get to the town.'

'The town? What town?' the stranger said. The pebbles crunched under his boots as he came down to the river bank. He was wearing a waterproof jacket and an old pair of jeans. He was foreign, but did not give the impression of being a tourist.

'The nearest town,' the lieutenant said.

'There aren't any towns round here,' the man said. 'There's an Indian village two days' walk away and a squatters' settlement not too far from there. What happened to you?'

Something among the mule's panniers shone in the sun: the blade of a machete.

'Any roads?' the lieutenant said. 'I could hitch a ride.'

'Oh, too far, too far,' the man said and stroked the mule. 'Where do you come from?'

7

'The town. I have to get back. If you could take me there . . . '

'Well, I can't take you there,' the man said impatiently. 'Where's your unit?'

'I want to get across.'

'The river? Why? You won't make it. The current is too strong.'

'Is it easier to cross somewhere else?'

'No. Nowhere close by.'

The lieutenant pointed at the mule. 'Perhaps if you helped me across — on the animal?'

'She can't carry us both. Why do you want to get across? The forest goes on for hundreds of miles on the other side too. You a deserter?'

'What? No, no.' The lieutenant stared at the river. His arm had begun to hurt badly again. A tree went floating by, and on the opposite bank a large bird stood flapping its wings. He said, 'I have to get going.'

'Don't worry,' the man said. 'I won't turn you in. It doesn't matter to me, one way or the other. Are you hungry?' He pulled the mule closer and took out some food.

The lieutenant waited with dignity to be given something to eat. The stranger handed him a few pancakes, and he ate them standing up.

'I've been following you for a while,' the man said. 'At first I thought you had come from across the border. I assumed you were a smuggler or an immigrant. I come across them now and then.'

The lieutenant finished his food. 'If you told me which way to go . . . ' he said. 'I suppose you know the way?'

'To the Indian village? I'll take you.'

'No, the nearest town.'

'You won't make it there on your own.' The man searched the mule's panniers and handed him a canteen. He said casually, 'Got separated from your comrades, eh? When was it? You were going round in circles, you know.' He had the manner of someone accustomed to observing others, as if he were about to pass judgement — a teacher perhaps.

'I'd be indebted to you if you took me to the town,' the lieutenant said. 'I am an officer.'

The man shook his head dismissively. 'I have to go the rounds of the villages, and I'm already behind my schedule. It's hard to travel with these storms. In the village you'll find someone to take you to the town. I'll ask the Indians to help you.'

'Is there a telephone there?'

'A telephone? In the village?' The man looked at the lieutenant mockingly. 'No, no telephones out here.' Then his expression changed: he had noticed the bloodstain. He asked, 'Are you hurt?'

The lieutenant nodded.

'You fell?'

'No — a bullet.'

'Caught in an ambush?' The man said in a worried voice, 'When was it? Whereabouts?'

The lieutenant made a vague gesture in the direction he had come from. It appeared casual, a show of bravado, as if an ambush was something ordinary to him — or, simply, he had no idea where it had happened. The stranger said, 'Is your wound serious? Let me see. What's that thing under your shirt?'

'A tourniquet.'

'There is a doctor in the village,' the man said. 'Well, of sorts. But he's better than no doctor at all.' He came closer and looked at the bloodstain on the shirt. 'Oh, it looks bad.' He examined the wound, through the hole in the shirt, in silence. The torn flesh and crusted blood did not seem to revolt him. He could pass for a doctor if he had not said already that he was not, somebody you could trust with your weakness.

'I'd rather try to get across the river,' the lieutenant said. 'The guerrillas may still be around.'

'You are as likely to come by them over there.' The man went to the mule and came back with a clean shirt and a pair of trousers.

'Put them on, in case we run into them. Do they know you've run away?'

'No . . . I don't know. They haven't come after me.'

'Have they taken any prisoners? They might tell them about you. At least you should get rid of your uniform. Take it off, you don't need it. We'll burn it. Otherwise some animal might dig it up.'

He fetched a gas stove and set the clothes on fire in a pile on the ground. The new clothes were small for the lieutenant. He looked lost and much younger without the uniform, more out of place in that corner of the forest than the foreigner. 'You a teacher?' he asked.

'What?' The man gave a little nervous laugh as if he had heard something absurd. 'What makes you think that?' He unzipped his jacket a little and the clerical collar attached to his ordinary checked shirt gave him a sudden authority. 'I can't go round the forest dressed in clericals,' he said. 'My name is Thomas.'

'You are foreign.'

'English. I studied in Madrid for a while.'

'What are you doing out here?'

'This is my parish. The whole of the forest.'

'Isn't it too large for one priest?'

'It's really very small, in terms of people, just a few Indian villages. But because they're so far apart I spend most of my time on the mule.'

'You go to the squatters too?'

'If I did, the Indians would stop coming to my church. Someone else from the town goes to them once every couple of months. Oh, it's all very political, I'm ashamed to say.'

The river purred by under the noonday sun. They waited until the fire burned itself out, and the priest scattered the charred remains with his boot. There was something unintentionally violent about it, like desecrating a grave or kicking a dead animal. When there were no signs of the fire left, he took the mule to the edge of the river to drink. 'So far there hasn't been any rain today,' he said. 'With a little luck we'll manage a few hours' walk without it.'

'Can we go back?' the lieutenant said. The priest did not seem to understand. 'To the place where the ambush happened. Someone may be alive.'

The priest shook his head. 'There won't be anyone. The guerrillas will have taken away those who could walk. Are you new here?' he said. The mule jerked and the man pulled firmly on the reins. 'When did you come to the south?'

'Three months ago.'

The priest looked across the river. 'Well,

you haven't been here long enough. Let's go. You are in no condition to lose any more time. The damp isn't doing your wound any good. It's getting infected. You don't want to lose your arm.' He began to walk, pulling the mule behind him.

The lieutenant stood reluctantly on the river bank. He said, 'If I was going round in circles, that place could be on our way, no?'

'Don't think about it. You did what you should have done. You are alive.'

The lieutenant said feebly, 'I have a duty . . . '

'What do you want to do?' the priest said. 'I'm not staying here any longer. Go back if you like. It'd be madness, though. You have no idea which way you came from.'

The lieutenant did not insist, and the two men and the mule followed the river upstream, walking in silence. The river had overflowed its banks, and their feet sank in the mud. A crocodile was sunning on a rock and the lieutenant grabbed a stick, but the animal did not stir. They came to a shrine: it was not unlike a wooden shed, a little like those shrines dedicated to the dead of some car accident one saw on the roadside all over the country. Someone must have come by boat to build it and probably had never returned. Behind its rusty grille there was a statuette of Our Lady of Guadalupe, a toppled vase with plastic flowers and a dusty votive lamp. The lieutenant crossed himself and moved on, speculating about the dead: someone who had drowned, his body never recovered perhaps. The thought filled him with dread, helplessness. Death had been an abstract notion until the day before: it had been his first firefight. His feet moved in and out of the soft deep mud, making an ugly noise. A snake slithered slowly across his path, as unafraid of him as the crocodile had been: he was the trespasser there, he ought to be careful and keep his distance. Ahead of them the mule neighed a few times — maybe something had scared it too. They turned away from the river and entered the forest along a narrow trail choked with ferns, and the priest had to use his machete. They stopped for the night while there was still some light, and set up camp on the edge of a clearing. The priest said, 'I have only one hammock. You sleep in it. I'll make my bed on the ground.' His strict voice permitted neither objection nor gratitude.

When it started to rain he had their little shelter ready. He put the rain sheet on the mule and tethered it a little farther away, then came back and got the stove out to make tea. He fixed a tarpaulin between two trees and they sat under it as the storm built up. The lieutenant drank his tea and thought of his men. They had all been very young, even younger than him, so similar to each other that he had had trouble telling them apart. Álvarez, López, Mendoza, Vargas . . . For a long time he had not been able to put faces to those names. The mule dipped its head into its nosebag, the monkeys quietened down and darkness came slowly towards them from across the clearing. The memory of the convoy making its way down from the mountains under the warm rain and the fading sun flashed into his mind: his men sitting in the back of the trucks with their heads bowed, his driver whistling a tune, the gunner leaning back on the turret of the armoured Panhard to let the rain beat against his face. Was his name García or Gutiérrez? The pain in his arm flared up, and he waited for it to ease before asking the priest, 'Do you live with the Indians?'

'Yes.'

'You trust them?'

He nodded. 'Of course, trust is understood differently here, just like religion.'

'Aren't you a Catholic?'

'Oh yes, of course. What I mean is that they have a tough faith. Well, perhaps that's how it should be. Christianity was always going to

be too timid for these parts of the world
. . . Do you believe yourself?'

'I suppose I do.'

'If it hadn't been for the conquistador's
sword, the Christian faith would never have
taken hold among these people,' the priest
said. He drank his tea with his head bent,
staring into the cup. His manner had
something secretive or solemn about it: a
priest bent over the altar, preparing the
Communion wine. The unsmiling lips, the
pale face, the yellow hair were like a mask.
The real face was hiding behind it — one
could only guess at what it looked like. He
said, 'In fact their version of Christianity still
has little in common with ours. I pretend not
to notice, of course, but I know they worship
their old gods with as much devotion as they
pray to Jesus. Only instead of religion we call
it tradition.'

'They are like children.'

'Oh, well,' the priest said, 'someone from
the time of the Conquest might have said
— without bad intentions, perhaps — the
same thing. He wouldn't have understood a
people who are simply different from us.' He
looked at the mule: it was eating quietly,
swishing its tail at the flies hovering around.
For a while he was quiet, as if he had
forgotten what he was talking about in the

wet humid evening. Then he said, 'It's arrogance to think ours is the only way that people ought to live, don't you think? They aren't children. They are as grown-up as you and me. Perhaps they are even wiser than us in some ways. The forest has taught them things we modern people struggle to grasp.'

'You think I'll be safe there?'

'In the village? Oh yes. Don't worry, they are polite.'

'Polite?'

'Yes, polite. They will look after you because they will know it's important to me. It's their way of thinking. Even when they disagree with me, they pretend to be persuaded, and I pretend to believe them.'

It was dark now, and the priest took a gas lantern out of his luggage and lit it. The sky had cleared up. The big grey clouds had moved on, and the stars had come out. The priest sat with his back to a tree and the tin cup of tea in his hands. The forest was as loud as in daytime, only the sounds had changed. The gas lantern stood between the two men, giving off a blue-grey glow, and the mule stamped its hooves and snorted. There was a sense of peace, the wind had died down and the rain cleared the humidity in the air. It was difficult to believe that men lay dead in the dark somewhere out there.

'You must be crazy to leave your country to come to this place,' the lieutenant said.

'Oh, my country . . . ' The priest made a little gesture as if shooing a fly: it was enough to erase a whole continent from the map. 'I don't miss it. This is my home.'

'Why here?'

'Oh, vanity perhaps? I thought that I could make a difference. Or maybe I did it for myself. Does that sound any less conceited? One way or another, the salvation of my soul doesn't matter.'

On the edge of the glow of the lantern the mule lifted its head in the rain and snorted. Sweat collected on the lieutenant's forehead and he shivered with fever. His wound had stained the shirt that the other man had given him.

The priest put his jacket over the lieutenant's shoulders. He said, 'You aren't well. You have to rest. We have a long walk ahead of us tomorrow.' He finished his tea and made his bed on the ground. 'We have to get to the village before dark. You can't spend another night out in the forest. Your arm needs looking after.' He helped the young man into the hammock and hung a mosquito net over it, before lying on the ground himself.

He fell quickly asleep. The lieutenant lay in

silence, listening to the rain and the priest breathing noisily and the mule chewing with its nose deep in the bag. A sense of failure came over him in the dark, and shame. It was not how an officer ought to feel. His legs hurt from the long walk of the last two days. The hammock swung with a creaking noise, and a little wind blew, carrying over the smell of wet earth and a spray of rain. The mule took its nose out of the bag and stamped its feet a couple of times, staring in the direction of the clearing.

He had left his men behind, the lieutenant thought. What else could he have done? A sharp jab of pain in his arm made him wince, and his doubts were dissolved by the selfish desire for survival. He could not see well in the dark, but his whole upper arm was clearly swollen. He touched his wound uncertainly: he was taken aback at the size of the swelling. He thought with horror about losing his arm. Getting to the village did not guarantee anything: there was no proper doctor there, the priest had said. He zipped up the heavy jacket, but it did not warm him up. The temperature was dropping, it felt to him. The mule snorted and took a couple of steps back and forth. He wished it would quieten down: he could not sleep. He thought of the shy corporal who had been his driver. Had there been enough time to think about home as he was dying? Maybe there had been a girl he had loved in another part of the country. He wondered what might have led him to join the army: a family tradition, some sort of idealism, the good pay . . . It could not have been a love of guns, he was not the type. Well, he should have taken a job as a waiter in a resort, where his politeness would have earned him large tips and his boss would have loved him because he worked hard, was never late and never complained. And the gringas would have been attracted to his curious eyes, his copper skin, the way he said 'bitch' instead of 'beach' or 'estation' instead of 'station', and how he would always remind the children to stay in the shallow end of the pool.

The forest had turned silent and the mule had stopped fidgeting. It had raised its head and was standing still. Suddenly it tried to make a dash for the clearing, but its tether jerked it back by the neck, and it began to swing its head from side to side, desperate to free itself from the rope. The animal's behaviour seemed comical to him until he saw something moving with great speed in the undergrowth. The jaguar came out of the grass and grabbed the mule by the neck with its claws. The mule bucked and kicked with its hind legs, but the jaguar hung on. The lieutenant began to shout and the priest woke up, but the cries did not scare the jaguar off. It had bitten the mule on the neck and was holding onto it with its teeth. Only when the priest ran towards it with his machete did it release its prey and go into the forest.

The priest put his hands on the mule's neck. The rain fell on, soaking his shirt and his face and washing the blood off, but more gushed from the wound. 'What should we do?' the lieutenant said.

'There's nothing we can do. She'll die.'

'We're still far from the village, no?' He watched the priest pouring water slowly into the mule's mouth. He said uncertainly, 'I came across it — the jaguar. Before we met.'

'Did you?' The priest gave him a look and stroked the mule's head, frowning, biting his lip, fighting back his anger under the falling rain. He did not look like a priest, with his wet hair plastered to his head and his fierce eyes. He said in a low voice, 'It was following you, and you brought it here.' He continued to stroke the animal, whispering to it in English. Then he said sharply, 'What are you doing here? Go and lie down.' He waved the lieutenant away, saying with vague bitterness. 'There's no reason for you to be here.'

'When I get to the town, I'll make certain

you're compensated, Father.'

The priest said nothing. The lieutenant went back to his hammock. After a short while the priest came and began gathering his things. 'We have to sleep somewhere else,' he said. 'The jaguar will still be around.'

'And the mule?'

'Let the jaguar have it.'

They carried everything to another spot on the other side of the clearing. At dawn they heard the jaguar returning to the mule. The priest lay on the ground, awake. It was not raining. The wind blew from the direction of the river, rippling the dew-covered grass. The clouds stood heavy and low, and soon it began to rain again, the drops tapping against the leaves of a banana tree nearby. The two men set off, with the priest going ahead with the machete. Back in the clearing the jaguar watched them go. It had dragged the mule to a bush and sat guarding it. The priest opened his way with the machete, walking without looking back. He felt a bitter dislike for the man he was helping. He did not fool himself that he was a good man. Suddenly the rain stopped. One moment it was pouring and the next not a drop was falling. It was one of those things that seemed almost supernatural to somebody who was not accustomed to the weather in the forest, but not to him: he

plodded through the mud and the mosquitoes, thinking of other things. This was
the land of the God of the Old Testament,
of wrath and the lack of mercy, a Garden of
Eden that had gone to seed. He did not mind
it — in fact he preferred it to England or
anywhere else. He would never go back.

2

Milagros knelt down next to the slab lying on its side. It seemed just like any rock covered in moss and dirt, but those were hieroglyphics carved on the limestone. She scratched the dirt off the surface with her fingers and tried to read the eroded relief. Something set her apart from the Indian in the tatty wide-brimmed hat and the plastic sandals who stood behind her, grinning. It was not his dark skin: there was some Indian blood in her veins too. Unlike him, she was educated. Good diction and correct grammar transformed a face more than surgery. She asked him to fetch the equipment and watched him go away. One could not see the Greek, the Celt, the Roman, the man of the Renaissance, not even the Victorian on a white face, for Western civilisation had moved too fast to leave any telltale signs of the past on the European skin. She thought: the white face is without history: too familiar, too unremarkable — always modern. But a look at an Indian face sends the mind travelling back a thousand years. The Olmec, the Maya, the Toltec, the Mexica were still there in the

24

coppery skin, the prominent nose, the high cheekbones, the epicanthic fold, the brown eyes staring back from the deep well of time.

Their mules were at the bottom of the hill. It was past midday and the humidity hung heavily in the air and did not let the body sweat. One could hardly escape it, day or night: like grief. The Indian came back and set up the surveying equipment, whistling cheerfully. He said, 'The sun's angry today, eh, señora?' An iguana plodded about, watching them without fear, unaccustomed to the danger of human presence. Milagros stood on the edge of the hill and watched the vast dense carpet of trees where a river snaked through. There could be whole cities buried out there without anyone knowing — not even the Indians? She suspected there were some who would not tell her if they knew. An eagle soared in a circle above: perhaps it had spotted a prey. There was a sense of peace in the silence that surrounded her, and a warm feeling stirred in her. She gave it a guarded welcome: happiness carried the threat of disappointment with it. She raised the binoculars to her eyes.

'This is a great day, señora,' the Indian said. He believed in happiness the way one believes in a god, without justification.

'What do you think will happen if there is a

lost city out there?' Milagros said.

'We'll get rich, señora.'

'Do you want to get rich, Moisés?'

'Yes, señora,' the Indian said solemnly. 'Very much.' He stood in the midday sun, a small older man with perfect teeth, looking at the landscape indifferently. 'I will build a house. Just like those in the town.'

Somewhere in the forest a column of smoke rose up in the sky. Milagros said, 'What's that over there?'

The man stopped smiling. 'The squatters, señora. They are burning down the forest again.'

He fell silent while she scanned the forest with the binoculars and the sun stretched the human shadows downhill. The air was growing even more humid. 'I was looking for you yesterday evening,' she said, looking through the binoculars.

'I had work, señora.'

'There seemed to be no man left in the village.'

'The jaguar.'

'You went to kill it?'

'Yes, señora.'

'Did you find it?'

The man shook his head. 'It knows we're searching for it.'

'I should think it better to set a trap.'

'Yes, well, it's too clever, you see.'

'Maybe you scared it away for good,' Milagros said, 'and it won't come back.'

'Oh, it'll come back. There's food for it in the village. Much easier than hunting for it in the forest.'

She trained the binoculars on a hill whose regular shape rose above the landscape: it could be a buried pyramid. 'Do you think it's a danger to people?' she said. 'I'd assume a jaguar could easily attack someone on their own.'

'Only other animals,' the man said.

'Not even a child?'

'The children have been told not to go into the forest.'

'Has a jaguar ever come to the village before?'

'No, never, señora. It's because of the squatters, you see.' He pointed at the forest and said, 'That's the jaguar's home. The more they burn, the less land it has to go hunting.'

'Isn't the army supposed to turn out the squatters?' Milagros said.

'The army is useless. They don't know the forest.'

'Some in the village think you should do the army's business yourselves.'

The almond-shaped eyes looked slyly at her. 'It's just talk.'

27

'From what Onésimo has told me, I gather they are talking seriously.'

'Venustiano's boy? Oh, he likes to make up stories. Don't listen to him, señora.'

'Well, he's not just any boy. He's the village head's son.'

There were a few scattered clouds, and their shadows slid over the uneven green landscape as they moved slowly across the horizon. The village was somewhere over there: a clutch of one-storey houses with earthen floors and palm roofs in a small clearing. One of the simple houses was Father Thomas's church, and there was a god-house of the old religion nearby too. She did not know where. In other places it was an ordinary house among the other houses of the village, but this one was hidden in the forest. The Indian went away and came back with the food. He served the young woman first, and then spooned some food onto his plate too. He took his plate and sat down a few feet away out of respect, picking at his food. He always ate very little. He gave the impression of somebody who did not care for material things — a saint. His ancestors would not have understood the concept of sainthood: their religion had many gods, but no saints. He believed in the Christian God and the santos, His saints, but he had not given up on the ancient gods, either.

After lunch Milagros went for a walk. In the forest the monkeys let out deep guttural growls. The trees were wet and the earth was soft, one could sit or lean nowhere. Not long ago she had thought of giving up and going home, even though she did not want to: this discovery meant that she would have to stay much longer. It was a relief. She brushed against the ferns as she went deeper into the forest of the mammoth trees shrouded in bromeliads. A supple shape stirred in a tree and a pair of staring eyes caught the light. For a moment they seemed human to her: sad, curious, shy: it was a monkey. The way it looked at her made her feel like an intruder. She did not belong to the forest with the muddy river and the villages with the small palm-roofed houses and the constant rain, but she was going to stay for as long as she could, like a stubborn unwelcome guest who refuses to leave.

It was the last jungle in the whole continent, still big enough for jaguars to live in it. From where she stood she could see the column of smoke from the squatters' fire rising above the tall canopy of cedar, mahogany and cypress trees. They were clearing land to plant corn, and later, after a few harvests, when the soil had become exhausted, they would turn their plots into cattle pasture. The Indians who were supposed to be the legal owners of the forest were against the farms, but the poor squatters were many more than the Indians and were protected by a band of guerrillas. The Indian came up to her and announced with his inexhaustible cheerfulness, 'Father Thomas is coming, señora. He is with a stranger.'

They returned to the mules and saw the two men coming from the opposite direction. Father Thomas raised his hand from afar.

'Where's the mule, Father?' the woman said.

He told her about the jaguar attack. The Indian listened anxiously. 'It was some distance away,' the priest said. 'We've been walking since daybreak.'

She said, 'It came to the village too. It killed a cow.'

'Anyone get hurt?'

'No.'

She looked at the stranger in the ill-fitting clothes and the ashen face. He seemed very ill. Under his shirt his arm was bleeding. He looked away as if he felt embarrassed about his injury. 'Did the jaguar hurt him?' she asked.

'No, no,' the priest said. 'We have to hurry. I knew you'd be round here. Can we borrow your mules? It would take us too long to walk to the village. I'll send them back with someone as soon as we get there.'

The wounded man was still looking at the ground, grim-faced, while the Indian went to saddle the mules. Milagros assumed that he had been injured in some accident — a car crash on one of those unpaved roads which the storms wash away every year, a few months after being repaired. She said to the priest, trying not to look at the stranger, 'Is he very bad?' She could not resist having another look at the red patch on the man's sleeve.

'He's losing blood. Are the mules ready, Moisés?'

The Indian was also curious about the lieutenant. He kept looking at him while preparing the animals for the journey. His curiosity turned into suspicion: he was not happy. He said quietly, 'Almost ready, Father,' but did not hurry up. Suddenly he said, 'He's a soldier,' while he fastened the saddle on the mule's back. 'Why are you taking him to the village, Father?'

'It doesn't matter what he is,' the priest said. 'He needs help.'

The lieutenant stood there, saying nothing. He seemed unsurprised: he was used to the hostility of civilians. Now and then the three people glanced at him and went back to their conversation while the mules swished their tails and snorted. The sun was beating down, but the scorching heat was just a little inconvenience compared with the pain from the wound. The priest said, 'Well, we shouldn't be wasting any more time.'

'Yes, Father,' the woman said, 'you'd better get going.'

The lieutenant sat on the saddle and held onto the reins, precariously balanced. The Indian and the woman watched them go; the lieutenant could not tell what they were thinking. He tried to imagine how it would feel to die. The pain, the loss of consciousness . . . People talked of a sense of peace, but they had not truly died of course. He could only think of it as an unbearable loneliness with nothing to do for ever afterwards. At least he would not be feeling any pain, he assumed, shivering with fever.

*   *   *

They did not travel fast. It was some distance to the village and the priest did not want to exhaust the borrowed mules. The landscape was always the same: mile after mile of mahoganies, giant ferns and magueys. The path ran along the edge of a lake where they stopped to water the animals. High cliffs shielded it from the winds and there was not a ripple on the brown-green water. A few solitary birds pecked at the mud on the bank, and an eagle glided around high above, then let out a cry and flew away. The priest led the mules to the edge of the water. The wounded man stared at him with feverish eyes. There was a small muddy shore nearby where a dugout lay rotting away. The priest had seen it when he had come that way before. He always wondered to whom it used to belong. He imagined an old Indian fishing in the lake until one day he had fallen ill and not returned. Perhaps there had been no children to follow in his footsteps — or they had gone to live in some town beyond the forest. The priest got back on the mule, and the two men continued their journey.

He thought about the possibility that the soldier would die before they got to the village. Having to dig a grave reminded him of how one year in school he had been given the role of one of the gravediggers in *Hamlet*. He could still remember the lines: 'Come, my spade. There is no ancient gentlemen but gardeners, ditchers, and grave-makers: they hold up Adam's profession . . . ' It felt like an incident from someone else's life. He had the reputation of being a wit back then. He could not identify with the insolent, quick-witted

33

boy that he remembered. It had been so long ago. 'But age, with his stealing steps, hath claw'd me in his clutch . . . ' It made him feel foolish to be whispering the lines to himself. How conceited he would have sounded if the lieutenant had heard him. He kicked the mule gently, up a grassy slope.

The wind picked up as they came to another path and followed it downhill. The mules kept their heads down, sinking their feet in the mud. There were no tracks: no one had come that way recently. The priest wondered what he would do if they came across the guerrillas. They knew who he was, of course. Their paths had crossed a few times in the forest, but they had said very little to each other. He did not matter to them, he was a curiosity: an English priest in a place where neither priests nor foreigners were relevant. Their faces bore the kind of discontent that leads one either to revolution or to God. He knew that expression: he used to see it in the mirror in his seminary days.

There was smoke rising where they were headed. He would have preferred to avoid passing through there, but it was the only way to the village. An hour later they came to a clearing filled with smoke, and the priest had to get off the mule and pull the two nervous animals through the burning fires. A group of men with machetes and axes were cutting the shrubs to guide the fire where they wanted it to burn. They were not Indians. They stopped and watched the two men approach. The priest raised his hand in a greeting: they did not return it. One of the men said, 'Who are you?'

'He is the foreign father,' an old man said, and took off his cap. 'Your blessing, Father.'

The priest said curtly, 'The Lord be with you.' The fire slowly burned its way into the forest, leaving behind tree stubs and earth covered in soot. He stared at the malnourished, unfriendly faces. 'Corn or grazing?'

'Grazing, señor,' the old man said, and put his cap back on. 'We have enough corn sown.' He spoke with civility but not reverence. Even after all those years it still felt a little odd to the priest not to be treated with the respect he had grown accustomed to back in England. He did not believe that he deserved respect, of course, neither now nor back then, but he used to accept it with complacency. The rest of the group seemed annoyed by his presence and stared back at him with a sort of contempt. The old man said, 'And where are you coming from, Father?'

'The mountains.'

The man nodded knowingly. 'Where are you headed?'

'The Indian village.'

'Ah, of course. If you wait a little, we'll give you a cup of coffee, señor.'

'Thank you. We have to get going.'

The old man looked curiously at the lieutenant. Father Thomas quickly asked, 'How much will you burn?' He rubbed his eyes, which were smarting from the ash. Even he had a farmer's hands: soft skin and perfume belonged to a stone cathedral, not to the hut with an earthen floor that was his church. The fire crackled as it swallowed tree after tree of the vast wild forest, and the air rippled from the rising heat. Birds fluttered about, dazed by the smoke.

'As far as the hills,' the old man said. It was quite some distance away. He asked, 'How are your Indians these days, Father?'

'You know how they are. They aren't doing well. You are taking over their land.'

One of the younger men said, 'With your permission, señor, the forest is for everyone.'

The old man silenced him with a gesture. He was of a generation that still felt some respect for a man of the cloth: the kiss of the hand, the bending of the head, the miraculous healings performed by some saint: he had grown up with all that. 'Well, señor,' the old man said, 'we are stealing no one's land.' He pointed at the blazing forest. 'They have

36

more land to themselves than they could ever use. We have nothing.' He drew his comrades' attention to some flames that had started to burn away from the main course of the blaze, and they quickly went to bring it under control by beating the front of the fire with branches and hacking at the bushes with their machetes. The old man said, 'Who is your friend, Father?' He called to the lieutenant, 'Good afternoon, señor.'

The lieutenant balanced uncertainly on the saddle with his eyes shut.

'What is the matter with the gentleman, Father?' the old man said.

'He's fallen ill.'

'Has he been on the mule long?'

'A couple of days. He's from the town.'

'Ah. A priest too?'

'No. A friend. He wanted to see the forest. Unfortunately he isn't used to the climate. The rains and the mosquitoes are too much for him.'

'Ah, he should have waited until the rains stopped,' the squatter said knowledgeably. 'This place isn't fit for townspeople.'

Father Thomas said, 'Quite. Well, he needs to lie down.'

They talked as if the lieutenant were not present, the way one speaks about a little child in his presence. The old man continued to look at the young officer keenly. He said, 'He looks very sick. Listen, Father, why are you taking him to the Indians? They won't be able to do anything for him. You go to our people now. They have medicines. Our place isn't far, you know.'

'I know. Thank you. He's not all that bad. And I have my own medicines in the village.'

The men returned from beating the flames, covered in soot and dripping with sweat. They had the sort of faces in which one could see anything one wished: malice, desperation, pride, mere exhaustion. The wind blew the heat of the fire towards the small gathering. One of the men said sullenly, 'Don't you have to go, señor?'

'The way to the village is through there,' the priest said, and nodded in the direction of the fire.

The old man said, 'The father and his friend are welcome to stay as long as they like. If you need to rest and something to eat, Father . . . ' He shrugged without regret. 'I'm sorry you have to go the long way, Father. Try the path that goes round the hill.'

'You don't need so much land,' the priest said. 'Aren't you too few to farm all that?'

'No, no, we'll bring in cattle and machines,' the old man said. 'We'll plant beans and maize, use fertiliser. Don't you worry now,

Father, we'll take care of everything.'

'Did you have to come so far away from your settlement?'

'Oh, the land around it is good for nothing any more.'

'How long will this whole business take?'

'The clearing of the land? Two, three days. We aren't going home until we finish it.'

'Are you going to sleep in the open? You should know that there's a jaguar around.'

Another man said, 'We're not afraid of the jaguars,' and shook the machete in his hand, playfully. His comrades laughed. The old man said politely, 'It won't come near, not with this fire burning, you see? But thank you very much for your concern, Father.' There was smothered laughter again. The old man ignored it. He asked, 'Have you heard about the ambush, Father?'

'What ambush?'

'An army convoy — far from here. Near the river. The guerrillas were waiting for them. It happened three days ago.'

'How did you hear about it?' He asked casually, 'Has anyone survived?'

The old man looked at him for a moment. 'I don't believe so, Father.'

'Poor men.'

'They've gone to hell,' a man said.

'I don't feel sorry for them,' the old man

said. 'You see, Father, the army burned our last village. We had nowhere to live for months. We slept in the rain.'

Father Thomas said, 'And the answer is to kill them?'

They did not answer him. Instead the old man said, 'You didn't come by them, did you, Father?'

'The soldiers? No.' The priest climbed onto the mule. He said, 'A jaguar can't live in a small patch of forest. You know that. One day there will be no animals left here at all — or trees. Have you thought of that?' He took hold of the reins of the lieutenant's mule and tugged at it. The two animals began to walk. The old man said, as if reassuring a child, 'The Lord be with you now, Father. And don't worry. Like I said, we'll take care of the forest and the animals.'

The two riders went slowly towards the thick forest, away from the raging fire.

3

Venustiano oiled his rifle, sitting on a rocking chair outside his house. He whistled and rocked back and forth, a young man with long black hair and a lean stubborn face, dressed in a loose white tunic out of which emerged a pair of naked brown feet. The very old bolt-action rifle with the long barrel had a new stock: he had carved it himself out of wood from the forest. A dog came up to him and sniffed at his toes, wagging its tail. He ignored it with an air of detachment. He did not want to give the impression that he was enjoying its presence even though they were alone.

The house stood a little higher from the rest in the village, but it was otherwise indistinguishable from them: all of a similar size, with wooden walls without windows, a palm roof and an opening at the front for a door. Next to the houses was an area of the forest which had been cleared and used for farming. Nothing had changed there since he was a child — with the exception of the house of the foreign god that the father had built. He did not like to think about his childhood, it had not been a happy time. The only good thing about it had been his grandfather. It was he who had first told Venustiano the story of Creation, how in the beginning there had been only one god who made the earth, but the earth had not been firm and there had been neither trees nor stones because God had made only earth and water. Then he had made the sun . . . He wondered whether his grandfather would have been proud of him if he were alive today. The Indian felt a great sense of responsibility: he was his people's leader.

The village was quiet at this time of day. The other men were farming, and he ought to be in his plot too. He was not going to go. He never liked being a farmer. He believed that the gods had created man to be a hunter. His grandfather had not told him any such thing, but he was convinced that it was true. The dog wagged its tail and yapped: it sounded as if it were mocking his earnestness. The boy, who played with the dog, was not there. The Indian thought about his son: the right to be the head of the village would be his legacy to him. It was not little, he thought, not little at all for a man to leave to his son. He tried the bolt a few times, then held the unloaded rifle against his shoulder and took aim at the houses in the distance: they looked small and flimsy: a big storm could wash them away.

A woman came out of the house. She was taller than him but much younger, with a narrow face and sinewy arms. She wore a cheap flowery dress and had her hair in a long plait, which was decorated with toucan feathers. The man said without looking at her, 'Where's the boy?'

'At Hesuklisto's house.'

'Is there going to be a ceremony tonight?'

'In the morning.'

'Why?'

The woman said quietly, 'The father will ask Hesuklisto to help the sick man.'

'Fine. We'll take him to the god-house after that.'

'The father says he might die if you move him.'

'He might die one way or another.'

'Isn't it better to keep him here?'

'Here?' The Indian made a grimace as if he had heard something absurd. 'We are risking our lives for nothing. The father shouldn't have brought that man here.' He went back to oiling the Mauser. He said that he had to oil it every day to keep the metal from rusting in the wet tropical air, but he seemed more like someone stroking an animal on his lap. The rifle had been his grandfather's; he had given it to his father, and now it was his. It was more than eighty years old — he did not know exactly — but it worked well and was accurate enough to hit a target at a great distance. He had not killed a large animal yet, only wild pigs and birds, but one of these days . . . He said, 'At least in the god-house the soldier will be hidden.'

'The father says he would have died, if he had left him in the forest,' the woman said.

He knew what looking at him sideways like that meant: she was keeping something from him. He did not say anything. He knew that she would tell him before long. Down in the village a group of children in white tunics ran and pushed each other playfully, making noise. He could not see their faces. His boy might be among them. No, he would not be: the woman had just said that she had sent him to clean the house of the foreign god.

'He is an officer,' the woman said.

'Is he?' Venustiano said and put down the rifle. 'I thought he was an ordinary soldier.'

'The father told me.'

'An officer is an important man,' the Indian said reflectively. 'Then we definitely have to hide him. The father should have asked my permission before bringing him here. He's disrespectful and careless.'

'The father says he'll go and get help from

the town. He says we ought to help him. The army is on our side.'

'What has the army ever done for us? The squatters are still here. No one's on our side.'

'He is only a young man.'

'A white man,' Venustiano said. He picked at the crust of mud between his toes with irritation. 'We've always done what the white man told us to do.'

There was no animosity between them. He knew she was proud of him — proud that he was the head of the village. The woman said, 'Have you decided about the cow?'

He said casually, 'Oh, I'll buy another.'

'When?'

'I can't go to the town now. It'll take me five days to get there and back. There is work to be done in the field. When that's done, I'll go.' In the village the children still ran about. Their distant voices reached him like the music of a song whose words he once knew. They were carefree, mischievous, happy — nothing like him at that age: he had been the village head's son, and a certain solemnity had been expected of him. The woman said, 'The squatters' camp is only a day's walk away.'

'I'm not going to go to any squatters' camp. I'll go to the town.'

'They would sell you the cow for less than in the town.'

He began to clean the rifle again under her silent gaze. He did not like the way she looked at him: it made him feel like a child. The woman said, 'We need a cow. We should buy one soon.' She added cautiously, 'Perhaps if I went to the squatters myself . . . '

'You stay where you are,' Venustiano said with hollow anger.

'They won't hurt a woman. Give me the money and I'll go. I know how to bargain.'

'I keep telling our people not to do any business with them, and now you . . . '

'I'll say I bought it in the town.'

'They won't believe you.'

'I'll go and stay with my sister for a few days. Then I'll go to the camp. No one will know.'

'What a foolish plan,' the Indian man said. 'It won't work. You'll shame me.' He shook his head dismissively. It was a matter of pride — how could they do business with the people who were taking over their land? Of course it would make no difference: the squatters were not in great need of his money, they sold their crops and cattle in the town, but his family needed a cow and the woman, it was true, could drive a hard bargain. The noise of the children playing went on in the distance, indifferent to the man lying close to death in the house of the foreign god. He rubbed the rifle barrel with feigned airiness while waiting for the woman to protest against his decision, but she stood there, fumbling with her cheap flowered dress in silence, giving him no excuse to relent and let her go: it annoyed him that she knew him as well as he knew her.

'Well, do you think you can do it?' he said tetchily.

'I will go tomorrow,' she said without any sign of glee.

'But don't tell the boy anything.'

'Oh, he's bound to make up some story.'

'As long as it isn't the truth.' He did not want to say any more about it. When he talked at length about things they seemed to lose their importance. A secret had a certain power to it: one drew strength from it. It was why the gods had secrets — from what he knew of the foreign religion, even the white father's little god had them too. 'And be careful,' he said. 'The jaguar is out there.'

'Yes.'

He stood up and walked down towards the village. There was a slight air of menace in his casual manner. He was like a farmer on his way to his field, but that was a gun — not a rake — over his shoulder.

4

The church was a house like any other with the addition of a wooden cross on its palm-frond roof and a small bell hanging from the eaves. There were no streets in the village. The houses — in reality nothing more than a couple of dozen large huts — were built in no particular order on the uneven ground, and the church stood among them without any authority or significance. Its interior was as unremarkable as the outside: a few benches made out of rough planks arranged on an earthen floor and an ordinary table to serve as the altar. A door led to a small room: the sacristy and the priest's living quarters. A boy with long black hair was sweeping the floor with a bamboo broom, making almost no noise. He might have been helping in a shop where business was slow. His Indian cotton tunic was speckled with mud, and so were his naked feet: he had never worn shoes. He looked down as he made his way slowly across the room, stifling a yawn conscientiously. The sound of children playing somewhere came in through the window without panes and the boy paused to listen, leaning against the broom. A dog was barking in between the sound of the football being kicked. After a while, the noise grew more distant and he returned to work. When Father Thomas came in, the boy hurried to kiss his hand.

A smell of mothballs spread across the room when the priest opened the wardrobe and hung his jacket next to his vestments. He had only one set of clerical clothes, which he carried from village to village for services, but even that seemed to him an indulgence — a piece of theatre. The older he became, the less patience he had for the rituals of his office, but the immateriality of the soul was a concept as abstract as pure mathematics: no religion would have been popular without its pomp and idols. How inspired it had been to turn faith into a trap for the senses: statues and relics, divine music, the Host, and nothing lifted the burden of reason like a whiff of frankincense. The boy kept stealing glances at him. He said, shyly, 'Is it true the señora discovered a lost city, Father?'

'Is this what they say in the village, Onésimo?'

The boy hesitated. He had a suspicion what he knew might be some kind of sin: one never quite knew what the foreign god permitted. He paused and asked, 'Have you been there yourself, Father?'

49

'Yes.'

'Then you must have seen it.'

'I'm afraid I didn't stay long enough to have a look around,' the priest said. He looked at the boy, who had been sent by his mother, no doubt, to clean his room. He was very unlike his father: he could not imagine the shy gaze and the easy-smiling lips on Venustiano when he was that age; in fact the boy looked like his mother. He wished that he had something to say that would please him. He knew how most people in the village hoped there was an ancient site nearby: then the tourists would come.

'Moisés says they found a statue,' the boy explained. 'They couldn't lift it. Not even with the mules.' He went back to sweeping the floor, but his mind was still on the mysterious discovery in the forest. The priest sat on the bed and stretched out his legs. 'The señora and he will go back tomorrow,' the boy said. Suddenly there were voices outside, and a group of children stampeded into the church. They peered through the door to the sacristy: boys and girls in dirty white tunics and long untidy hair. They did not expect to find the father there, and they blushed — perhaps: you could not tell for sure with the dark Indian skin. Someone grinned bravely at him: he was missing a couple of his front teeth. The priest thought: a dentist would have been more useful in this place than me; the torments of the soul could not compare with the agony of caries. Onésimo looked at them with craving eyes, but he had not finished the job he had been ordered to do. He said, 'I can't come.'

The children went away. The priest felt sorry for the child, but it would have made no difference if he sent him away: his mother would blame him for it and send him back another time. She would have come herself if she could, but she was a married woman and people would gossip. It seemed absurd to the Indians that his god did not allow him to have a wife. Venustiano did not like his wife looking after the priest. He distrusted the foreigner and his faith, thought of him as an enemy. 'What sort of statue was it?' Father Thomas said. 'It must have lain there for a long time.'

'Yes,' the boy said. 'From the time when our people ruled the forest and the places beyond.'

'The señora must be pleased.'

'I don't know, Father. She keeps very quiet. Perhaps she doesn't want people to know.'

'Why do you say that, Onésimo?'

'If the squatters find out, they'll steal the place from us.'

'How does one steal a whole city?'

'It's no different from the rest of the forest,' the boy explained earnestly. 'They'll go and set up their camp over there, then say they'd been living there all along, and demand money from the government to let it dig out the buildings. They could make money out of the tourists too. There'll be nothing left for us.'

'I'm sure the señora won't let that happen,' Father Thomas said. A sense of hopelessness came over him — there was nothing he could do for these people. They tilled the land the way their ancestors had been doing for hundreds of years, and they still hunted with spears and bows — only Venustiano had a gun. How long would they survive like that? Perhaps the boy would be living in the town in a few years, working in a factory, wearing Western clothes. He remembered when he had first come to the village, how charming it had all seemed to him: their simple way of life, their contentment, their disregard for wealth, their lack of curiosity about the world beyond the forest. The men worked in the fields and the women did the jobs in the house and the garden. There had been no violence until the squatters had come and built their shacks near the streams and sowed any flat piece of land they could find. The Indians did not like it, but simply avoided them. Then more squatters came and kept coming, and they all needed land too, and that was when they began to set fire to the forest. So the Indians had gone to the government, and the army had been sent to evict the squatters. But the outsiders were still there, and had even set up a little army. Now the problem for the government was not so much the squatters as the guerrillas. The priest felt sorry for the squatters, but it was the Indians that he supported. The dry fronds of the roof crackled with the first drops of rain. 'You should ask the señora about her discovery, Onésimo,' he said. 'She'll be happy to tell you, I'm sure.' A smell of rotten flesh blew in through the door and made him wince. He said, 'Is the cow still out there?'

'Yes. Father says the smell keeps the jaguar away. Will you say Mass tomorrow?'

The rain tapped loudly against the roof. A few drops came through it and fell onto the floor and the furniture. Father Thomas said, 'Yes. Tell your father to bury the cow. I don't think the smell matters to the jaguar. It'll be worse in the morning.'

The boy nodded. 'Are you going to pray for the soldier, Father?'

'I will.'

'You should ask Hesuklisto to help us with the jaguar.'

The priest said, 'I hope you'll pray with me too.'

'Can Hesuklisto really make the jaguar go away?' The boy's eyes were fixed on the priest.

'He just might.'

A drop fell on the priest's face. It felt like a tear: he had not cried since he was a child. He was not certain that he was capable of it any more. It was one of those abilities one loses when one grows up, like believing in fairy tales or entertaining yourself with a stick or a piece of string. He wiped the raindrop away and looked at the village out of the window. The people went about their business without hurry, as if it were not raining. He said, 'Do you like coming to church, Onésimo?'

'I do, Father. But I don't understand much.'

'Don't worry. It takes time.'

'I want to understand.'

'I know. You just have to be patient.'

The boy said, 'I can read the words. It's just that I haven't come across those particular ones before. Mother says it's because they're Hesuklisto's own words.'

'Well . . . '

'That's why they're so difficult, no? A god doesn't speak like an ordinary man.' He leaned against the broom and stared at the priest.

'You understand enough,' Father Thomas said. 'Don't worry about the rest. They're just words. Try to remember the things that we discuss. The rest you'll forget sooner or later. They'll vanish like drops of rain.' He stood at the window of the small room and looked out at the rain. There was no point confusing the child.

'When will I get to eat the little piece of bread, Father?'

'You have to learn just a few more things before your first Communion.'

'I know more about Hesuklisto,' the boy said airily, 'than any grown-up in the village. But they get to eat the bread, and they didn't have any lessons.'

'Don't mind them. The lessons will make you a good Christian.'

'Are the others bad Christians, Father?'

'No, no. But I suppose they may have doubts. If you know your catechism you will be able to understand better the word of God and have fewer doubts. Well, one hopes so. You can go now, Onésimo.'

The boy gave him the broom gladly. 'Goodbye, Father.'

The priest watched him skipping away into the village under the rain, glad to be relieved of his dull task. How oppressive the church must have seemed to the boy, he thought. Love, sin and sacrifice, the body and blood of Christ, the afterlife: all that must have meant nothing to him. He only understood what it was to be happy.

★ ★ ★

The cow lay in a field next to the pen where the cattle were kept. A barefoot girl in a white tunic sat on a corner of the fence, keeping watch over them: it was her duty to raise the alarm if the smell of rotting flesh did not keep the jaguar away. Her important assignment was dull, and she kept turning to look at a group of children playing noisily some distance away. The smell did not bother her, not even when the wind blew it towards her and the houses of the village. The priest greeted her as he walked past, and she nodded with an inexpressive face, not smiling back: an Indian smile was a reaction of great joy, not mere politeness, something rare and precious, not to be offered without a good enough reason.

He came to the land used for growing crops on the edge of the village. In spring the Indians set this land on fire and afterwards planted in the fertile ash-covered soil, not

56

wasting an inch: papaya and maize, rice, tobacco, sugar cane. There were some men there and he greeted them too, getting the same cool response. He went on, leaving the village behind and entering the shaded forest where the air was a little cooler. Soon his trousers were covered in mud: it was impossible to walk without dirtying them, so he turned back. Hortensia, Onésimo's mother, always offered to wash his clothes and cook for him, but he declined. He had hoped that the Indians would appreciate his not taking advantage of his position, even on something as slight as that, but it had been one of many occasions when his good intentions had had the opposite effect: they thought of him as aloof and mistrustful. If only he could make them understand — but even speaking their language made no difference. It was as impossible as explaining British humour to them. He had tried to tell some old jokes after Mass once, so that they did not think of him as distant and formal, but the deadpan delivery and self-deprecating sarcasm had alternately puzzled and dismayed them.

He returned to the church. In the back room, apart from the wardrobe, there was a camp bed with a thin mattress and a small folding table with a single chair. He felt protected in there, well hidden — from what? It was guilt that had brought him to the forest, but he had not escaped from it. At least it seemed easier to be virtuous here. The everyday tasks of life — to feed oneself, to bathe, to find a place to sleep, to travel — left him little time for introspection, and virtue lived in the mind, not the body. This place was satisfyingly foreign to him: the Indians with their language and way of life and the landscape and the weather — even the tropical diseases, which ordinary medicines could not cure, he suffered with a mix of curiosity and contrition. How different this place was from his old suburban London parish.

His former life seemed so trivial now — an affluent community interested only in itself: the raffle and the bazaar and the patron saint's fair. He had been so complacent there. Everyone had liked him and thought he was a great priest. In the end they had infected him with their smug confidence. He remembered how one time word had come to him that a married woman in his parish was having an affair. He listened to the news with a frown, nodding gravely, but really taking great delight in it — what a hypocrite he had been. The following Sunday after Mass, when he stood at the door of the church greeting his parishioners, she too came to shake his hand, but he turned away from her without a word.

It had been so satisfying — to reject a human being like that.

He sat on the edge of the bed and scraped the mud off his shoes. Then he noticed the plate wrapped in a banana leaf on the table. It was heaped with food, which had turned cold: the boy must have brought it when he had come to clean the room, but forgotten to tell him. His mother was one of those people who believed that to be a good Christian one should above all be good to a priest. He dried his face and went out again. Across the village he entered a house carefully, trying to make no noise. An old man sat on the floor, busy with something. He said in a low voice, 'How is he, Ernesto?'

In a corner of the room the lieutenant lay covered with blankets on a mat. 'He's sleeping,' the Indian said. 'I gave him something to drink.'

When the priest's eyes got used to the dim interior, he made out the sick man's face. He had a calm expression, but under the hard stubble his skin glistened with sweat and his breathing was fast and erratic. His feet jutted out from the short mat: even that little nakedness gave him an air of vulnerability. They were not the hard-crusted feet of the Indians with calloused toes: Father Thomas imagined the man's soles starting to bleed after a few steps barefoot in the forest. He said, 'His arm?'

The old Indian shrugged and returned to his work. He had a wooden mortar between his legs and was crushing seeds with a pestle. The priest lifted the blankets and looked at the injured arm: the badly swollen skin had turned almost black. He covered the sleeping man again and said, 'When are you going to move him to the god-house?'

The old man said, 'As soon as Venustiano tells us.' He beat down with the pestle, making a rhythmic noise. In the dark hut it seemed like he was playing a drum in a ceremony evoking a healing spirit. The priest watched him work. He said tartly, 'Why wait? You might as well do it today.'

'They have to make a stretcher.'

'Do you agree with it? Moving him in his condition?'

'We can't keep him here,' the Indian said, avoiding the priest's eyes. 'The people are afraid.'

'Of what?'

'Oh, you know, Father . . . '

'There is nothing to be afraid of, Ernesto,' the priest said. He stood in the middle of the hut, his head almost touching the beams supporting the roof. He was not a tall man, but the Indians were all very small. The wooden pestle tapped in the dark. He said, 'God is pleased with what you're doing for this man.'

'Is he, Father?' the Indian said doubtfully. 'Is Hesuklisto really happy?'

'I am sure he is. Don't you remember any of the things we've talked about in church? How one ought to love and help others — even his enemies? The army isn't your enemy anyway, is it?'

'No, no. But this soldier's coming here can't be a good omen.'

'You think so, Ernesto?'

The man looked up, anxiously. 'Hesuklisto sent him to us, didn't he, Father?'

'What makes you think that?' The priest moved a little closer so that he could see the old man's face as he sat bent over the mortar.

'Well, Father, you coming across him like that . . . and he being a soldier. It's like the stories you tell us in Hesuklisto's house.'

'I suppose it is. That is why — '

'And to happen now . . . '

'What is so special about this particular time, Ernesto?'

'I mean the matter with the squatters, Father. Is it possible that Hesuklisto sent him to us? To tell us something?'

The old Indian stopped with the pestle in his hand and gave him a keen look: it was the priest's turn to look away. If only he could believe in those terms too — but his faith was too abstract, too cerebral. He did not believe in omens, could not see God in the rain, the thunder, the grooved trunk of an old tree . . . It was starting to get dark outside and the men were coming back from the fields. The small houses already glowed with the cooking fires, and the air smelt of the dead cow. 'The Lord,' the priest said, 'has sent me. To help you.'

'Of course, Father,' the Indian said gloomily. 'We are grateful to Hesuklisto for having sent you to us. Please pray for us and this man.'

The priest returned to the church and slumped on the bed. A centipede serpentined on the wall, and the bats flapped furiously in the dark outside. He watched the centipede's move, and tried to guess which direction it would take next: it was like a game of chance, at which he lost every time he placed a bet. He thought of the lieutenant lying in bed too and of his chances of surviving: they were very slim. It was too hot in the room and he took off his shirt, but it was not long before the mosquitoes began to drone around his head and draw blood from his pale European skin. He lay still, telling himself that he should not care: a few doors away a young man was dying. But it would serve no purpose to catch dengue fever now. The net hung in a knot from a hook in the ceiling: the boy had tied it up when he had come to clean the room. He let it drop around his bed, then killed the mosquitoes that were trapped inside, wiped his hands on his trousers and lay down again. On the other side of the net the droning continued all night. He thought how ordinary life and horror were separated by a chance as thin as that nylon mesh. You do not realise how flimsy it is: one day it rips and you are on the other side. He shut his eyes and tried to get some sleep, listening to the mosquitoes and the fluttering of the bats outside. On the edge of the village the little girl, barely silhouetted against the mud-brown sky, still kept watch.

5

The god-house was a large palm-roofed hut hidden among the banana trees: one had to come very close to notice it. Venustiano left his rifle and machete at the door and went in. The hut was swarming with flies, and the air was still heavy with incense. Hanging down from the beams of the roof were the drums and the conch they had used in the ceremony of the previous evening. The lieutenant lay wrapped in a blanket on the floor, still sweating and shaking: the gods had not wished to help him after all, the Indian thought. It was in the god-house that his grandfather had told him that the end of the world would start with an eclipse. The lord of the underworld would wake up and cause an earthquake by kicking the pillars of the earth, the ground would split open and out of it the great jaguars would come to eat the people. The earth would turn very cold then because there would be no sun, and the trees and all the plants would die too.

His grandfather had been a wise man, he thought, but his father had betrayed their people by abandoning their gods to become a Christian. Even the Spanish name that he had given his son felt like a curse from which Venustiano could not escape. He remembered how his father always carried on him a book some missionary had given him. On the cover had been a blond wraithlike Hesuklisto lovingly putting his arms around a man with his face in his hands. There had been more colour illustrations inside: a shepherd coming to the rescue of a sheep standing on the edge of a cliff; a crying woman surprised in her room by a vision of God; an exhausted white man in a pith helmet down on all fours, a trail of his footprints in a sandy landscape with a glaring sun . . . The message of hope was easy even for an illiterate Indian like his father to understand. Most of the people had followed his father's example (he was their leader after all) and converted too. When he had died and Venustiano had become head of the village, he had persuaded them to go back to worshipping their old gods, and now the foreign father was trying to make them change their minds again, even though he pretended to respect their religion.

Venustiano had guarded the sick soldier all night, and now he waited for the man who would be replacing him. That morning he had briefly gone out to kill some game, but had not come across anything. In his grandfather's day one only had to walk a few minutes from the village to kill a monkey or a deer — and just with bow and arrows. How things had changed since then . . . Perhaps the end of the world was not so far away after all. He sat down with his back against one of the poles supporting the roof and nodded off, listening to the weak breathing of the man beside him. He dreamed that he was a boy again and his grandfather was teaching him how to shoot. The rifle was too heavy for him, and the old man had rested it on a pile of stones. Venustiano was kneeling down and holding the stock against his shoulder. A group of men from the village had gathered to watch, and they were teasing him. His grandfather said, 'Pay no attention to them,' and gently touched the barrel to stop it from shaking. The target was many yards away and Venustiano felt the weight of the gun. He paused to wipe the sweat from his face, and when he took aim he saw that the target was not a piece of wood but the faceless shadow of a man. He called, 'Grandfather?' but there was no reply. All he could hear was the men of the village giggling. He did not look up or lower the gun — it was as if something was forcing his finger to stay on the trigger. The man stood there, stock-still, his arms outspread like Hesuklisto, as Venustiano called again, 'Grandfather, grandfather,' and

66

his finger squeezed the stiff trigger . . .

He heard something and woke up abruptly. A weak voice said, 'Water', and he looked at the sick man. He had not moved, but his eyes were open. The Indian went over and lifted the blanket a little. The man's arm was terribly swollen and almost completely black. The wet bandage over his wound was held in place by a piece of bloodied string wound around it several times. The man mumbled, 'You the doctor?'

The Indian nodded and the man sweating under the blanket gave him a look of despair and contempt: a young barefoot Indian was not how he had imagined a doctor to be. He lay awkwardly on the mat, a tall thin man dressed in clothes that were too small for him. His eyelids were drooping and he was unshaven: it made his paleness seem even more pronounced. The Indian untied the string and removed the long piece of cloth covering the wound. He took from his pocket the pouch that Ernesto had given him and sprinkled the torn flesh with powder, then wrapped a clean cloth around it. The man watched him with blurred eyes for a moment and said feebly, 'Water. You have water?' and made an attempt to sit up, but fell heavily back on the mat. The Indian went to bring water.

A short distance away was a stream. He filled a bowl from it, and sat for a moment listening to the noise of the flowing water. He breathed in the fresh air: there was a purity in forest life — disease and death belonged to the world beyond the forest. It was the outsiders who brought these evils, he was convinced of that. He returned to the hut and helped the man drink, appalled at how hot his skin felt to the touch. The yellow eyes stared at him without gratitude, just with the greed of a man clutching on to life. After a few sips the man gave up. 'You want more?' Venustiano asked.

'No, no more.' The Indian laid him back on the mat. 'Where am I?' the lieutenant said.

'You are well hidden here. It's better than in the village.'

'Where's the priest?'

'Why?'

'He brought me here. I need some help . . . '

'He can't help you. Neither he nor his god. You believe in Hesuklisto, no?'

'What the hell are you talking about?'

The Indian took out the pouch and sprinkled some more powder on the bandage. 'He's at the village,' he said. 'He's going to go to the town to get help.'

'How long will it take him?'

'To get there? Three to four days.' He put the pouch back under his tunic and sat on his haunches, staring at the sick man with harsh, rude eyes — a curiosity seemingly without compassion. He waved his hand to drive away the flies circling his head and continued to stare. He said, 'Are you sure the guerrillas aren't looking for you, señor?'

'No, no . . . '

'Because if they found you here, it'd be very bad.'

'They think . . . I'm dead,' the lieutenant said.

'But can you be sure?'

'The priest will help me.'

'Oh, the priest, the priest . . . ' the Indian said. 'Did he tell you he runs this place?'

The lieutenant winced and his hand instinctively went towards his swollen wound, but stopped before it touched it, like someone wanting to pet an animal, only to change his mind at the last moment, thinking it might bite. He lay on the floor with the blanket wrapped around him. Every now and then he let out a moan and his hand squeezed the blanket. The god-house was filled with his suffering. The Indian thought it was an insult to their gods to have a white man in there. Perhaps he should not have brought him there after all. The temperature rose as the hour moved closer to midday. The flies buzzed over the sick man and sat on his face, but he did not bother to drive them away. The forest outside was quiet: it was like the animals knew there were people around and were keeping their distance. Suddenly the man began to cough. Blood trickled out of his mouth as he coughed. He demanded, 'Give me water.'

The Indian felt a sudden rush of resentment. He was the head of the village. No one had the right . . . He gave the man the bowl and sat back, watching him sullenly. The lieutenant had a few sips and lay down again. The Indian watched him fall asleep. It seemed to him that he would be sleeping for a long time, and he picked up the rifle and the machete and went to search for game again. He had gone a long distance from the hut when he heard a curassow calling. He followed the sound, stepping carefully over the twigs and roots, becoming more careful the closer he got. He waited until the curassow would stop its call, and then he would take a few soft strides forward, searching the trees with his eyes: it was difficult to make out the bird in the permanent gloom of the forest. When he was very close and it called again, he saw its bright-red wattle among the foliage: it was on a high branch a short distance away. He raised the rifle, but the bird moved behind the trunk of the tree; perhaps it had sensed the danger. He waited for it to show itself again, and when it did he quickly steadied the gun against his shoulder and fired. The bird dropped to the ground with a weak flutter of its wings, a little splash of life going out in the forest. A feeling of bleakness stirred in his heart as he picked up the soft, shapeless body with rough fingers and held it in his palm. Its head hung down loosely and the warm blood dirtied his hand. Death came easily, it was as random as a gust of wind: you could not predict it. Only the gods knew. He slung the bird over his shoulder and took the path back.

Near to the god-house he heard low voices coming from inside: they were not Indian. He listened for a moment in dismay, not knowing what to do. He could not go away. He left the bird at the door and went in, his bare feet making no noise on the earthen floor. A group of men carrying sheathed machetes stood over the man lying on the floor and were talking to him. They had their backs turned to the Indian, but he could tell they were squatters. The smell of soot from their clothes was all around the hut: the smell of a forest fire; it was as bad as the smell of a rotting carcase to him. The squatters were asking the man on the floor questions, and he was answering them truthfully. In his fevered confusion he seemed to think that they were soldiers. They listened and nodded, then asked him more questions and coaxed the answers out of him as if talking to a child. The Indian said, 'What are you doing here? Go away. This is a holy place.'

They turned round, startled and worried. Then they realised that the Indian was alone and took their hands from their machetes. An old squatter pointed at the lieutenant and said, 'What about him? How come he is in here? Is he one of your gods too?'

'We brought him here so that the gods would cure him.'

The old man grinned. 'They should hurry up, no? It seems to me he's dying.'

'Leave him alone. He needs to sleep.'

'Are you hiding him?'

'No.'

The group of men in jeans and boots stared down at the small barefoot Indian in the cotton tunic. The old man said, 'We heard a shot. Was it you?'

'Go away. You have no right to be here.'

'This man will die soon,' the old man said. Behind him the lieutenant mumbled something about being late and having to get back to the garrison. The squatter looked at him and turned back to the Indian and said, 'He says he is an army officer.'

'Let me see your papers,' the lieutenant said.

'He doesn't know what he is talking about,' the Indian said. 'He's very sick.'

'Is he a friend of the priest's?'

'No.'

'We saw him with the priest a few days back.'

'I don't know.'

The lieutenant called behind them, 'Sergeant! Bring me some water.'

'He was wounded at the ambush, wasn't he?' the old man asked. 'It seems to me you are hiding him.'

'Where's the sergeant?' the lieutenant went on. 'Tell him I want to speak to him. We are late.'

The men looked at him. 'I don't know who he is,' Venustiano said. 'The father found him in the forest. He said he had had an accident.'

'You Indians are filthy little cowards,' one of the other squatters said. 'You have the army to do your dirty business, don't you? Well, this one won't be doing any more harm. He is going to hell.'

'Let him die in peace,' Venustiano said.

'The guerrillas should be told. Don't go

hiding him someplace else now, you hear? You'd be wasting your time anyway. The comandante will make you tell him where he is.'

'This is our land,' Venustiano said. 'Go away.'

The delirious voice said, 'Sergeant! Send three men to check those huts.'

'Let's go,' the old man said. 'We have to get back.'

'What about him?' another man said, pointing at the lieutenant.

'We'll tell the comandante.'

They went out, but the smell of soot lingered in the hut: it felt like an insult that had gone unchallenged. The Indian went to the door and said aloud, 'You are trespassing. You should apologise.' For a moment they were speechless with disbelief, then began to laugh at his indignation. A barefoot young man in a loose dirty tunic was not deserving of their respect: dignity and pride belonged to trousers and a shirt, a pair of shoes and a face with something European in it. Even their enemy lying on the floor commanded more respect than he, the head of the village, a descendant of kings, Venustiano thought. He called out again, 'Come back and apologise!' but they walked on, laughing, with their backs turned to him. There were four of them, and

74

the gun was loaded with the only clip that he carried that day. There were four rounds left: he had used one on the bird. He bolted the rifle and took a couple of steps forward. The arteries in his neck throbbed, as if someone had had his hands around his throat. He decided on the order in which to shoot them without hurry — they were not walking fast. Their heads were no longer human, just a few easy round targets he had to hit, much easier than killing the curassow. He stopped thinking and raised the rifle and fired, then bolted it and picked his second target. The first man went down without a sound, and his comrades stopped and looked at him, stunned. The Indian fired again and another man fell. It was ridiculously easy to kill a man, he thought. The last two squatters broke into a run, but the muddy ground sloped up and they could not get away fast. He fired two more times, aiming at their heads, and they rolled down the slope one after the other.

He put the rifle down, feeling a curious calm. The forest had turned silent during the shooting, and it was now beginning to fill with sound again, covering the memory of the incident like shovelfuls of earth over a corpse. Venustiano stood with the rifle lowered and thought: I am the forest — for a moment he felt as if he had grown out of the earth himself. A monkey howled somewhere deep in the trees, repeatedly, but got no reply: the animal and he were the only witnesses to what had happened. They and the gods, of course: they ought to approve. He went back to the god-house. The sun had moved and the sick man lay in the shadow now. His face was wet with sweat, but calm, his eyes open, his cracked lips slightly apart. The Indian found the bowl of water — perhaps the soldier wanted to drink. He lifted the sick man's head and brought the bowl to his lips, but the warm dirty water trickled down his stubbly cheeks and onto the floor: he was dead.

Part Two

6

For a moment she was unsure whether she was awake, but the bed creaked as she turned on her side: dreams did not include trivial details like that. The glow of daylight showed through the cloth that covered the only window in the narrow room. She could hear distant voices and a dog barking, but even though the sound of rain had been constantly there in her sleep there were no clouds in the sky. Through the door she could see the palm-roofed house opposite: it seemed empty — then she noticed movement inside. A woman came to the door and stared at her with expressionless eyes from across the street. Milagros's throat felt dry and she went out to get some fresh water. More faces appeared from the dark interiors of the houses as she went past and stared at her like masks with holes for the eyes.

Sometimes she dreamed of a little house with a veranda where she could sit in the evening until it was too dark to see. Then she would go and lie in bed with someone and tell him what had happened that day and everything else that would come to her mind.

That would be happiness — and also to have a child. There was supposed to be plenty of time for all that, but her life did not seem to be going that way. Something would happen in a dream and she would wake up in the middle of the night, terrified, and then she would lie silently in the dark, holding a vigil of despair. She could resign her job and leave the forest. She thought of the jaguar: all those trite stories of people who had had a brush with death and how it had made them realise the preciousness of life . . . Hope flickered in her heart like a little fire, warm but frail: it could go out at any moment.

She was relieved to return to the coolness of her own house. It was really no more than a large hut: a single room with a table and a bed. The backpacks propped against the wall contained all her clothes, the metallic boxes next to them the surveying equipment. The books lined up on a crudely made shelf seemed out of place in a room with an earthen floor and palm roof. A long piece of cloth was nailed above the door, and she pulled it down, craving some privacy. In the dark she was reduced to a shadow, flickering with the flapping of the door cloth in the breeze. She caught glimpses of the village behind it, as if looking through the shutter of a camera: a chicken pecking at the ground in the blazing sun; a boy running past with a stick held like a submachine gun; clothes hanging from a line; the woman opposite staring at her. Her sombre face made Milagros feel uneasy.

She picked up a book and lay on the bed again. There was nothing else to do when the day was as hot and humid as that. Through the splits in the wooden walls she saw a small shadow moving soundlessly outside. It hesitated, then moved on, keeping close to the house. A moment later a small hand pushed aside the cloth hanging across the door, and Onésimo stood silhouetted against it. The woman pretended to be asleep, but watched him out of slit eyes. She wondered whether he would dare to come in. He had gone through her things before, more than once in fact, when she had been away with Moisés — she could tell with the uncommon perceptiveness that the solitary person has about their living space: the chair left slightly askew, the book spine sticking out from the row on the shelf, the sheet hanging a touch lower on the bed: they were as easy to notice as misplaced pieces on a chessboard at the start of a game. The boy took a couple of uncertain steps into the room and stopped, staring at her with his mouth open: his two upper incisors were missing. Then his eyes caught sight of something on the table. He went towards it, his bare feet making no sound on the earthen floor, turning back to glance at the woman on the bed. A propelling pencil lay on a map spread out on the table: he picked it up and went silently away.

The woman opened the book and began to read. An insect flew around the room, banging against the walls, searching for a way out, attracted to the light shining through the split wooden walls. The cracks were too narrow: freedom was an inch away but still impossible as it banged against the boards with mindless persistence. The woman turned the page and something fell out. She picked up the piece of the photograph and looked at it: a man smiling at the lens, his arm raised as if resting on the shoulder of a woman who was in the half of the photograph that was missing. The scissors had also cut across a child's head resting on his lap: a happy family holiday; but the woman had not been Milagros and the child was not hers. She had meant to come to the forest to put all that behind her, but you could not free yourself of feeling with a pair of scissors. She must have put the photograph in the book long before and had forgotten about it. What should she do with it? She could not throw it away: it would be like admitting there was no hope of ever being happy ... She put it back in between the pages. She looked up and caught a glimpse of the woman in the house opposite, still watching her from the shadows. A baby began to cry, and the Indian woman went away from the door. After a while the crying stopped, and the birdsong and the calls of the animals in the forest returned. Another woman came down the earthen street, carrying a large bundle of firewood on her shoulders. Milagros recognised Hortensia — a small silent figure in a long tunic, just out of adolescence but already the mother of a grown child. Childhood lasted so little time in the forest. It felt like an indulgence to have grown up in the city, to have been given toys and been cared for, to expect to be happy.

★   ★   ★

The priest was working on the hut that was going to be the school on a cleared piece of land on the edge of the village. Moisés was there too, sawing wood for him. The shape of the building, a rectangle little more than five yards wide by ten long, was outlined in chalk on the ground, and a few poles were already in place. There was a pile of stripped tree trunks nearby, and a large stack of palm fronds drying in the sun. Some children had been there when the two men had started work earlier that morning, all excited and eager to help, but after a couple of hours they had begun to drift away. Father Thomas could see them at the other end of the village now, playing noisily some kind of ball game. They did not know what a school was — perhaps another house where the foreign god stayed, brooding in the dark and the smell of sacred smoke. The Indian man brought another armful of wood and helped the priest stand a tall pole straight up in one of the holes dug in the ground. He said, 'Aren't you going to go to the town, Father?'

'There is no hurry now,' the priest said.

'Yes, of course,' the Indian said, as if apologising on the priest's behalf.

'I'll go soon — next week perhaps.'

The priest filled up the hole around the pole with the spade and pressed the loose earth down with his foot. The light of the sun rolled over the roofs of the village, and the shadows of the houses stretched out towards the fields where the maize had been left to dry. There was something welcoming to the eye about the neat rows of stacks: a sense of order in the apparent confusion of the forest.

'And buying a new mule, Father?' the Indian said. He spoke without looking at the priest. It would be presumptuous of him to tell the father what to do. In a day or two it would be impossible to take the dead man away: he would rot before they reached the town. So he is going to bury the soldier in the village, Moisés thought. He did not like that. The dead had the power to hurt the living, if they thought they had been mistreated in life: and the people in the village had not done enough to help him.

'It can wait,' the priest said.

'Perhaps that man had a family,' the Indian said, picking up another pole and standing it up in another hole.

'I will let the authorities know when I go.'

'Sure,' the Indian said. 'You know best, Father.' He held the pole straight up and said, 'It's just that it's very warm round here this time of the year. It's not good for the dead to — '

'I am going to bury him tonight.'

The dark face under the tattered straw hat turned towards him with an expression of surprise. 'Where, Father? It's not good burying him in the forest. Some animal would dig him out before long.' He nodded towards the trees. 'Would Hesuklisto allow it?' he asked with sincere curiosity. 'Our old death-gods wouldn't.'

The priest finished fixing the pole in the ground and put the spade down. It was hard working in the heat. He said, 'Venustiano gave me permission to bury him behind the church.'

'He did? Oh. If he says so . . . '

'I'll need some help,' the priest said. 'Will you help me, Moisés?'

'Aren't you going to take him to the town, Father?' the Indian said as if he had not heard.

'What good would it do him to be buried in the town?'

'Yes, of course, Father,' the man agreed promptly. 'It would be foolish to take him to the town. If you came across the guerrillas . . . '

'Will you help me dig the grave then?'

'Yes,' the Indian said. 'I am a good Christian, Father. You know what Hesuklisto desires. I am his servant — and yours.'

Father Thomas looked at him. There was great warmth in the narrow dark-brown eyes: kindness felt like an old, difficult-to-master craft that hardly anyone practised any more. He said, 'I am grateful to you.'

The Indian took off his hat and said, smiling, 'Your blessing, Father.'

The priest's hand rose and the dark face bowed in gratitude. A small crowd of children with long black hair and calf-length tunics formed quietly several feet away; they had stopped playing and returned to watch the building of the hut. They were mostly boys, but there were a few girls too — the eye had to rest on a face for a little while before it was able to tell. They stared back at the priest with dark unblinking eyes. In England one would call them rude, but here curiosity was not a sin of childhood. He waved them closer, but they stayed where they were. A short while later the sound of a flute — an unvaried repetition of the same notes, as if someone were trying out the instrument — lured them away again. The two men went back to work.

'What do you think about Venustiano, Moisés?' the priest said. He began to strip another tree trunk with his machete, trying to ignore the rising heat, pausing to wipe the sweat off his forehead. 'You know him better than I do.'

'He is the head of our village, Father,' the Indian said feebly. 'He worries more than the rest of us.'

'I know you have great respect for him,' the priest said. He felt a twinge of shame, asking questions about someone behind his back. But recently he had started wondering about Venustiano, wanted to know what sort of person the young head of the village was. He remembered him as a little brooding child when he had first come, as silent then as he was now, keeping his distance. He could not quite understand him. He looked at Moisés, a small simple man in a wide-brimmed hat and plastic sandals, kneeling down and sawing wood. He had been his first convert of sorts: Christian humility came naturally to him. At the same time, like almost everyone else in the village, he had not turned his back on the old religion and took part in the ceremonies in the god-house. To the Indian, the mud and the rain, the jaguar and the giant mahogany were gods too, whom he could see and touch, unlike such notions as love and self-sacrifice and eternal life; nature and violence were real, were felt by the senses. The priest said, 'The problem is that Venustiano doesn't say much about anything.'

'That is the way he always was.'

'I wish I knew what he thinks.'

'Nobody knows what he thinks. He isn't like the rest of us.'

'You mean his father . . . '

The Indian looked at him without surprise. 'I didn't know that you knew, Father.'

'All I've heard is that his father wasn't from this place.'

Even though he had lived among the Indians for so long, they kept their secrets and old faith well hidden from him. Nevertheless, little secrets like that trickled down to him now and then.

He said, 'Does he know the truth himself?'

The Indian shrugged. 'Well, what if his blood isn't pure? Whose is? No one minds.'

'I was told that his father wasn't from the forest at all.'

'He was someone who used to come here to tap the trees for gum.' The Indian picked up another stick and began to cut it. He said casually, flattered to know something that the father did not, 'He was working near the village and got to know Venustiano's mother. She wasn't married then.' He darted a look at the priest and went on pushing the saw back and forth. 'You know how it is, Father.' Then it crossed his mind that his story was insulting to the foreign god and his priest. He had had the vague impression that Hesuklisto disapproved of things like that; he did not want the father to think that he condoned such behaviour. He added, shaking his head solemnly, 'Very bad, very bad.'

All the poles were now in place. The priest began to fix the vertical boards to the ground and to nail them together: they would form the walls of the hut. There was a tenacity and patience in the long pale fingers holding the nails driven into the wood with light taps of the hammer. The noise travelled to the forest and was answered by a bird knocking its bill against a hollow tree: it was something of a consolation to be acknowledged like that. The priest moved slowly round the hut, keeping at his task, the nails clinking in the pouch hanging from his waist. He was reminded of a re-enactment of the Crucifixion that he had attended in the federal capital in his first years in the country. It was a piece of street theatre without any real violence, no mortification of the flesh, but one was slowly dragged into it. Some spectators even approached the man acting the part of Jesus to ask him for miracles. He promised to help them — maybe even he had forgotten who he really was — and the supplicants rejoined the crowd of onlookers lining the streets, glad to be given the divine promise . . . That sort of behaviour ought not to have surprised him, the priest thought: there was no more realism in the Mass that he said every Sunday himself.

He thought of Venustiano again, with his decrepit rifle and child bride and boy and small house, which stood out from the rest only because it was built on top of the hill. It was not a great distinction to be the head of the village; it was of his supposedly long royal ancestry that the young Indian was really proud. The priest said, 'Venustiano's mother must have been very young at the time.'

Moisés brought him more boards for the hut. He said, 'The man asked her father to marry her.'

'I suppose he refused him.'

'He agreed, but the man changed his mind. When he finished with the trees, he left with the rest of the gum-men.'

'It must have been terrible for the woman.'

'Well, Father, that's how the white man is,' the Indian said ingenuously. 'You can't trust him.'

'I remember Venustiano's father. I mean — the man who eventually married his mother.'

'He had wanted to marry her before all that happened. Of course her father told him she was going to have a baby. He didn't expect him to want her after that, but he did. He could have had anyone. He was the head's son, no? But he married her all the same.'

'He was a good man.'

'Before he began to drink,' the Indian said. The priest put down the hammer and wiped his forehead again. The sweat was running into his eyes: it was coming to midday and was getting too hot to work. The Indian went on with the building of the hut alone, without any sign of discomfort. One could not but admire his quiet strength: a small lean body that was used to the heavy humidity and the heat — or maybe he possessed the sort of fortitude one rarely came across in the world beyond the forest. The priest said, as if he were seeking some sort of concession, 'Shall we go back?'

The Indian answered obediently, 'Yes, Father,' and began to gather the tools and pieces of wood.

'Take the spade,' the priest said. 'We'll need it for the grave.'

He washed his hands and face, and studied the primitive little unfinished building. It seemed as if a little wind could blow it away. He did not worry: the storm season was over, and they could take their time to make the hut robust and waterproof like the rest in the village. They left, the Indian walking alongside him, spade in hand.

He said, 'People expected him to kill the baby. He had the right. You know, Father, things like that happened in the past.'

He spoke in a calm and unemotional voice: that was how it used to be, there was nothing more to be said. Sorrow and love and hatred were not there in his story. He did not dwell on what went on in the small wooden houses of the village; motives and justifications kept only the Western mind busy. The village stood still in the noonday sun, a few dogs wandering the empty streets and clothes swaying from a line. Smoke was coming out from the roofs of some houses and a machete fell repeatedly somewhere. The priest went on half-heartedly, not in the mood for what he had to do. He saw Venustiano coming from the opposite direction with his rifle slung over his shoulder. He had a sullen expression: it was the face of authority. He looked around as if inspecting the village, his manner full of an overblown sense of duty. When he came up to the two men he said, without a greeting, 'Father, are you going to do it today?'

'I am going there now. I will say a short prayer first. You can come too, if you like. It won't last long.'

'I can't come.'

'Well, never mind. Moisés has been kind enough . . .'

'Remember, Father, what we agreed. No name on the cross. You promised me.'

'Yes, I remember.'

'It's for my people's safety.'

'Of course. I understand.' Father Thomas thought about the dead man lying in the anonymous grave. It would be temporary anyway: when he went to the town he would let the army know where the lieutenant was buried.

'Their lives would be in danger if the

guerrillas came this way,' Venustiano continued unnecessarily. 'It isn't my fault he died
here. You didn't ask my permission.'

'Oh, it was my mistake. I will do as agreed.'

The young man left, and the priest and
older Indian went across the village. People
came to the doors of their houses and children followed them to the church, cramming
into the small room where the body lay on the
altar. They stared at it in silence while the flies
hummed around it. A little girl began to cry,
but the other children hushed her. The priest
began a prayer and promptly Moisés took off
his hat. He stood beside the priest, staring at
the body, feeling no emotion about something
that could not be changed; it was the sort of
resignation that made bearable a death in
childbirth or from an illness that incantations
and prayers had failed to cure.

7

A hoarding on the side of the road advertised a local brand of mineral water: blue waves and the happy light-skinned face of a woman who was not from the south, probably not even from the country. This was how everything was always sold: with a promise of escape. Among the crowds in the Old Town with the colonial houses, municipal sweepers in Day-Glo waistcoats cleaned the cobbled streets with bamboo brooms. A smell of ammonia travelled through the air, and a man came out of a public toilet without doors, casually fastening his belt; a caricaturist could reduce him, without much guilt, to a trimmed moustache, a head of sleeked-back hair and a gold ring. In the zócalo the baroque façade of the cathedral cast its shadow over the cafés filled with tourists and the square where a balloon-vendor paced up and down like a loyal sentry. A few locals shared the benches under the trees, staring idly about in the humid evening. They seemed as indifferent to the tourists as to the historic buildings and the Indian women selling rebozos and trinkets. On the steps of the cathedral a little girl sat herself on a tourist's knees and asked him coquettishly for money.

The hotel was in a side-street. Its false luxury annoyed the priest, but he returned to it every time he came to the town because it was cheap. He gave the bellboy who carried his bags to the room a few coins, and immediately the young man whispered the names of a few good restaurants, as if he were letting him in on a secret; he assumed the priest was a tourist. He went uncertainly away. A mosquito net hung from an elaborate rail over and around the bed. Father Thomas opened the window. Belfries rose above the roofs of the town, and in the far distance stood the blue-green rounded cones of the mountains he had come from. The air brought in the smell of pine.

Someone had forgotten a magazine on the table, and the priest sat back in bed and leafed through it. His eyes fell on an advertisement for some sort of software for Catholic confessions: 'A step-by-step guide to the sacrament . . . multiple-user support with password-protected accounts . . . choose from seven different acts of contrition . . . ' The minibar began to hum. It was a presence of sorts in the otherwise silent room — one of those subtle presences that go largely unnoticed, but still offer one a little company. Wherever he happened to stay he welcomed the dripping tap, the creaking bed, the humming fridge, the ticking clock (but the last was a memory of childhood: all clocks were digital now).

There was a knock on the door, and the bellboy stood timidly at it. He stared at Father Thomas, then asked how he liked the room and whether there was anything that he needed. He listened absent-mindedly to what the foreigner said while his eyes travelled across the room — that was not the reason why he had come. Then he looked at the priest and said, 'My boss says you are a priest, señor.'

'Yes.'

A motorcycle went noisily past outside, and the bellboy said, 'If you'd prefer a quieter room, Father . . . ' but the priest shook his head, and the young man went back to his gloomy introspection. It was as if he had wandered in by mistake, but did not want to admit it and was trying to think of an excuse for it. Father Thomas did not remember having seen him before.

The young man said, 'My boss says you live in the forest.' The priest's nod seemed to encourage the bellboy, who said, 'I've only started here last month, but my boss knows you well.' The minibar coughed and stopped humming, and the two men stared at each other in silence. The bellboy said, 'Can I ask you about it, Father — the forest?'

'What would you like to know?'

The bellboy said timidly, 'I just wanted to know how it is to live out there.'

'That, of course, would depend on where exactly you mean. The forest is a large place, you know.'

'Is it . . . safe?'

'Well, I'm sure it's more dangerous than living here.'

The bellboy eagerly waited to hear more, and the priest tried to think of something to satisfy him. 'There are parts where there aren't any roads. But I suppose you aren't thinking about living there. It'd be very difficult to get provisions if you did.'

'And there are wild animals,' the bellboy put in. 'One must be careful. Do you have a gun, Father?'

'Me? No. It's people who are more of a danger, to tell you the truth.'

'You mean the army?'

'You know, of course, that there's a sort of war going on in the forest because of the evictions.'

'They say the guerrillas protect the poor people from the army.'

'Well, I'm a priest. I'm not supposed to be taking sides.'

Immediately he felt bad for having said it: a stock phrase to avoid taking responsibility. He threw the magazine back on the table and smiled at the young man standing at the door. He was reminded of a child's confession: vulnerable and confused, opening up to someone who might let him down . . . The traffic quietened, as it was coming up to the hour of the siesta, and the music of a distant radio was heard in the noonday peace, persistent and cheerful like a tourist tout. The bellboy said, 'Father, my boss says you live with the Indians. It must be difficult . . . '

'Well, no. They are decent people.'

'I come across some of them in the market now and then. They've got shifty eyes. We don't trust them here.'

'They aren't any different from you and me,' the priest said, 'in matters of trust at least.'

'If you say so, Father,' the bellboy said, unconvinced.

'Why do you want to live in the forest?'

'Oh, I'm thinking of trying my luck there — farming some land.'

'Do you know anything about farming?'

'It shouldn't be hard.'

'Are you going to go alone?'

'I have a fiancée, Father,' the young man said solemnly. 'She works as maid for a family here in the town. She makes very little — like me.' Outside the open window the music slowly died down, but then another song began on the radio, even more exuberant and loud. 'It's not enough to live on,' the bellboy said. 'We want to have children.'

'Life isn't easy in the forest,' the priest said. 'You will never get to own the land, the forest will always belong to the state. That won't change. You might get evicted at any time.'

'Well, it's worth the risk.'

'What about your children?'

'Oh, they will be fine, don't you think, Father? We'll teach them to read and write.'

'The forest isn't perhaps the right environment . . . '

'It won't be for long, Father.' The man took the innocent comment as disapproval; he treated priests with the unquestioning obedience of a religious person. He added hurriedly, 'We'll send them back here when it's time to go to school, of course.'

'That would make sense.'

'We'll find a family for them to lodge with. One day, when we have made enough money, my wife and I could come back too.' There was a long silence and he seemed to realise that he ought to go. He said, 'Thank you for your advice, Father.'

The distant music had stopped mid-song: perhaps the owner of the radio was going to bed for the afternoon. Flies were circling the room and knocked against the glass of the other shut windows, while the smell of cooked food came up from the ground floor. The locals had abandoned the main square to go home, but the iron tables were still full of tourists dressed in shorts and hats, and at the doors of the old cafés the waiters stood drumming their fingers on their trays, sweating in the shade.

'If we go, Father,' the bellboy said, 'will you come and visit us sometime?'

★   ★   ★

A Dominican nun showed him to the far end of the cloistered courtyard where the bishop was sitting in the shadow of a potted orange tree. A stout man with a stubborn face and manicured hands, he took out a handkerchief, mopped his forehead and beckoned him closer. 'How long exactly,' he said, 'has it been since we last met, Thomas?'

'I believe six months, Your Excellency,' the priest said.

The bishop nodded pensively. 'It's very unhealthy to live in such humidity. I suppose it's worse in the forest, isn't it?'

'Oh, one gets used to it, I suppose.'

'And you being a foreigner . . . It must be even worse for you.' He barely paid attention to his visitor's remarks. He could not imagine that one's reaction to something as obviously bad as the weather in the uplands was a matter of opinion. He said, 'I wish I could move to the coast. I'm rotting here. To a northerner like me, this place is murder — murder.'

A phone rang somewhere, breaking the calm of the colonnaded cloister with its persistence.

The bishop said with a sigh, 'Oh, that rude invention.' He looked in the direction of the sound as if his stare could silence it, and in fact, after a moment, someone in a room out of sight picked up the phone. The bishop rocked in his chair, irritably.

Father Thomas said, 'Did you know that Graham Bell refused to have a phone in his study?'

'Is that a fact?' the bishop said without interest. 'I didn't know that.' His eyes looked over their heavy bags at his visitor. 'Why haven't you come to see me sooner?'

'I haven't been to town since we last met, Your Excellency.'

'Do you mean to say you haven't got my

letter?' The bishop rearranged his cassock carefully. 'You ought to find a better way to let me get in touch with you. A post-office box is no good in case of emergency. How long will you be staying?'

'I'm leaving in the morning. I only came to buy a mule.'

'What happened to the old one?'

'It was killed. A jaguar.'

The bishop did not show any surprise. He said, 'We will reimburse you. Remember to give my secretary the receipt before you leave.'

'There is also the matter of the army officer . . . '

'Yes, yes,' the bishop said impatiently. 'Someone's already told me about him.'

'What was it that you wanted to see me about?'

The bishop reached for the glass of water on the table next to him. Father Thomas could not imagine him ever being a man of ideals — but how often one comes across an old photograph and fails to recognise the younger self of a familiar face. Perhaps the bishop too had once promised himself that he would resist dishonesty and indifference, be charitable and serve the poor. The bishop said unexpectedly, 'In isolation, one is tempted to assume one can create one's own little world.'

'I don't understand.'

'Why did you come here, Thomas?'

'Here?'

'To the forest.'

'Oh, I was looking for a greater challenge than being a parish priest.'

'Where exactly were you before?'

'London.'

'You must be mad,' the bishop said unsmilingly, 'swapping London for this place.'

'I suspect you haven't been there, Your Excellency.'

'London? No, I haven't. But isn't there a saying about it? When a man is tired of London, he is tired of life, right?' The bishop chuckled.

'Oh, well . . . '

'I guess you had no idea what you were getting into. It wasn't what you expected, was it? Nothing like the photos in a travel guide. Am I right?'

'Well, I haven't regretted it.'

'Maybe it feels strange to be asked all this,' the bishop said, 'after all these years you've been with us. But I always felt I have no right to probe into my priests' private lives.'

'I don't mind.'

A young man in a plain cassock walked along the covered arcade on the other side of the courtyard. The sound of his shoes on the flagstones sounded rapid and official; one could imagine him being a deacon of great pride and ambition destined for high office. The bishop followed him with his eyes until the young man went out of view. 'I wouldn't have done it if I didn't think there was a problem,' he said. 'I want to understand you and your motivations, give you an opportunity to explain why your ministry has been such a — well, there's no two ways about it, a failure.'

The priest stood, stunned, in the shadow of the potted tree while the sun burned down in the courtyard. He thought of the village in the forest, the Indians working in the fields, the small church and the dead lieutenant. He tried to guess why he was considered to be a failure — but he could think of no reason to believe he had been successful. He said, 'I'm surprised at your harshness, Your Excellency. One can never be certain of one's shortcomings, of course . . . '

The bishop gazed at the garden. There were rose bushes round the statue of a saint standing with his hands pressed together in prayer. Father Thomas could not read the name on the stone from that distance. A bright-yellow bird chirped, balancing on the statue's head. 'Not being able to understand your failure is part of the problem,' the bishop said. He sipped from his glass of water while his eyes always observed the priest. 'What do you think my opinion of you ought to be?'

'Oh, how should I know ... That I'm foolish perhaps? A priest who hasn't earned his people's love.'

'If this were a matter of not being loved I wouldn't worry.'

'I suspect you think a priest ought to be feared more than loved, Your Excellency.'

'It's more helpful for what we're supposed to be doing, certainly.'

'What is that?'

'Why, our duty to the Lord, of course.'

Duty: it was one of those words that could so easily lose its meaning — like love; one had only to hand them over to the cynic. The priest wished he had not come. He said, 'I can reassure you that I am very committed to communicating the word of God to the Indians.' The bird on the statue was gone the next time he looked: without the little splash of colour, life had gone out of the saint; he became just a mossy, grim slab of stone. The light of the sun crept deeper into the arcade where the bishop still sat in the shadow.

'Don't you think you've gone too far with your innovations, Thomas?' he said.

'Is this about my trying to persuade the

Indians to say Mass without me and discuss the Bible among themselves? Then you should be pleased to hear that I haven't succeeded. It was impossible to convince them that by performing some of the duties of a priest they weren't committing some great sin.'

'Oh, I have no objection to all that. Some good might have come out of it, I'm sure. It's more what you teach them when you are present that worries me.'

The old colonial building was in a state of disrepair. Large pieces of green plaster had fallen off the walls, exposing the brickwork; the paint on the doors and shutters along the cloister had peeled off and the exposed wood was rotting; tiles were missing from the roof, which was covered with plastic sheets to stop the rain from leaking in: it was not a rich diocese. Father Thomas remembered the time when he had first met the bishop. It was a surprise to see how much the familiar face had changed over the years: the old brusque manner was still there, but did not quite belong with the grey hair and the blotchy skin. The priest felt sorry for him. 'I teach them,' he said, 'what I know. What the Bible says, Your Excellency. I can't shy away from the fact that the Bible sometimes contradicts itself.'

'You are confused, Thomas.'

The bishop stood from his chair and gestured for him to follow him to the garden, where someone was now watering the flowers. When the bishop came near, the man put down the watering can, took off his cap and bowed. The bishop made a vague gesture in his direction without pausing. 'Why do you let the Indians worship their gods, Thomas?' he said. 'You are undermining the credibility of the Church, everything that took men before you centuries to achieve.'

'I don't understand.'

'You allow them to go on believing Our Lord is just one of many gods.'

'Oh, that,' the priest said. 'Since I can't stop them from going to the god-house, I believe it's better not to go against their traditions. At least that way some of them do come to my church too. The problem is that they fear rather than love me. I am a judge of sins, I have the right to grant forgiveness and mete out moral punishment. I don't like it. I'm sure our faith wasn't meant to be like that — a religion of fear.'

'If I were you,' the bishop said, 'I would find out where the damn god-house is and burn it down. What next? Joining their ceremonies?'

'I wish they'd let me,' the priest said

frankly. 'I'm afraid they don't trust me enough.'

'Is this a joke?'

'Actually no, Your Excellency. Their rituals are hardly cruder than ours. Their meaning is the same too: obey the gods or be punished.'

The bishop grunted with disapproval. 'I'm beginning to guess why you really left England, Father.'

They were no natural allies, they just happened to be on the same side of faith; they were like two escaped convicts chained together who have to help each other if they are to make it to freedom. Father Thomas said, 'My old English parish was, I suppose, much like a small country. A very small conceited country, pompous and smug about its independence, but about which no one in the world gave a damn. I am a fugitive from it.'

A bird flew into the garden and perched on the ivy climbing the old walls. The priest listened to it chirp. He remembered how the bishop had said to him once, 'Thomas, I wonder what you really believe in,' and he had replied with sincerity. Perhaps it had been a mistake to be so open about his beliefs, which had changed so much over the years. He had said to the bishop then, 'What I believe in? I don't believe in the sort of Christianity that is all about anger. I believe divinity can't be separated from humanity.'

'That sort of talk will get you into trouble.'

'I suppose so. But I am unable to believe many of the things said about Jesus.'

'What things?'

'Oh, the miracles . . . In this day and age . . . Science has long made it impossible to believe in the traditional God.'

'These things are in the Bible.'

'Along with the cruelty, the vengefulness . . .' He had said, 'I no longer want to believe in a God who destroys his enemies, sends plagues and kills children. I'd like people to start looking for him beyond doctrines and dogmas, beyond religion even.'

'You don't believe in God?' the bishop had said.

'Oh, I still believe there is something holy about life — something other than the survival instinct. But I don't think of it as a miracle-performing deity, intervening now and then by overruling the laws of nature.'

'Do you think that limitless love would keep one alive round here for long? Or anywhere in the world, for that matter — other than on a desert island perhaps.'

'I hope so.'

'Science, for which you have so much respect, Father, says there isn't much love in nature.'

'Oh, no, there are many examples of altruism in nature. Not the same as love exactly, but not too dissimilar, either. An animal that will adopt an orphaned animal of another species . . . The monkey who gives alarm calls to warn other monkeys of danger nearby, even though in doing so it might attract attention and get attacked itself. Aren't they examples of altruism?'

'It makes sense to animals that live together.'

'People live in groups too. Anyway, the old way of talking about God is meaningless these days, completely irrational, in my opinion. It turns more and more people away from religion. Does one really have to believe in a Jesus who walked on water, healed the sick or raised the dead? Isn't it more important to believe in His radical humanity? That's what the concept of God means to me.'

'Just being a nice person? Is that all you are asking of those Indians out there?' the bishop said.

'Don't you think it's enough, Your Excellency? I understand your disappointment about my little gospel. You think it trivial, I suppose. After all, religions aren't really about the search for truth, but about security. They exist to nurse our fear of death, of nothingness. I am afraid I have nothing to offer for that. People don't want to hear that no god will come to save us. Salvation is the feeling of fulfilment. What we have to do to experience it is to offer our love to everyone, unconditionally. God is already here, within us. One only has to let him out . . . '

The bird flew out of the garden again. The priest followed it with his eyes. Yes, it had been a mistake to speak so openly. They came back to where the chair was. The bishop sat down, took a little bell out of his pocket and fingered its chain like a rosary. Then he rang it. The nun came silently. 'María,' the bishop said, 'this is Father Thomas.' The small heavy woman nodded from where she stood, several feet away, while watching the priest with caution. The priest suspected that the bishop had spoken to her about him, and she was now comparing him to the way she had imagined him. She did not seem that old, but the shadows of the cloister falling on her made less obvious the signs of old age on the coppery mestizo skin. The bishop turned back to the priest and said formally, 'The reason I wanted to see you, Father Thomas, was to let you know personally that I am relieving you of your parish.'

Father Thomas met the nun's eye. She quickly turned away and her pair of canvas shoes hid timidly under the hem of her white habit: it was as if she were trying to become invisible. 'Well,' he said, 'I didn't expect to hear that.'

'I am sorry I have to give you such bad news,' the bishop said and stretched in his chair.

'Would you allow me to appeal against your decision?'

'I didn't make it lightly, Father,' the bishop said with a shake of the head that refused the priest his request. In the courtyard the gardener was pruning the rose bushes round the saint's statue: the shears moved gently in his hands, as carefully as a barber cutting hair. There was something humble about committing oneself to such a simple under-taking — it was admirable to lack ambition sometimes, the priest thought.

He said, 'Where are you sending me?' He imagined a post in another remote part of the country. Perhaps he might be allowed to choose it.

'You are to go back to England, to be pastor to a convent,' the bishop said. 'It will allow you the time for prayer and reflection that I feel you need. I asked Sister María here to arrange it. She speaks English, you know.' The nun took half a step forward in her soundless shoes. The bishop said, 'I'm not good with languages myself.' For the first time that evening he smiled. It struck Father Thomas as a spiteful gesture.

He said, 'When do you wish me to go?'

'Oh, there isn't a great hurry, Father. Two months should be enough time to say your farewells to the Indians, don't you think? Come back by Christmas.'

Father Thomas bowed and went out. That part of the town was off the tourist trail and the streets were almost empty. A few boys kicked a can, and a pair of girls sat on the pavement passing a doll to each other in some game of motherhood. A moment later they moved on, taking their indomitable excitement elsewhere, far away from the horrors of the dinner table and the small shared bedroom. A light wind lifted the dust off the street, birds sat on a telephone wire and the exhaust of a car bumping down the cobbled street was heard over the evening peace. In a small corner shop two men leaned against the counter and an old woman sat fanning herself with a piece of cardboard. The priest said, 'Buenas tardes,' as he went past and all three gave him a reluctant little nod. They were still watching him through the door as he turned the corner. This was life in a provincial town: the numbing monotony, the intense pride, the anticipation that something important would happen, but it never did.

He went for a walk in the Panteón. A few women were cleaning tombs, a dog with swollen teats wandered round and the keeper was sweeping the gravel paths. The priest had not seen his punishment coming. He wondered who had told the bishop, who had never been to the forest himself, about the Indians and their still practising the old religion. He had not done it himself, guessing that the Church would not have liked it, but he had never thought it that important; it had felt like he had been left to do what he thought best in the forest. There could not be many who wanted to take his place. Then he remembered how a few months earlier a priest from the north had come to the forest as part of his tour of the south. It had to be him. Father Thomas had been surprised to have a visitor. The diocese had not told him about the priest, he had assumed that it had been a last-minute thing, and there was no other way to contact Father Thomas than the post-office box in the town. The man had stayed for a week, and they had had several discussions. Perhaps Father Thomas had told him about the Indians' rituals, he could not quite remember . . . What he did remember was how the visitor had asked him to celebrate Mass with the Indians. He had confided to Father Thomas that he was a recovering alcoholic, and they had said Mass together so that Father Thomas could drink the Communion wine afterwards. They could have used grape juice, but the man had declined, doubting the purity of the grape juice, which would become Christ's blood. How Father Thomas wished Christians would free themselves from the superstitions of another time . . . He would not have minded a post anywhere in the country, but did not want to go back to England.

He saw the cemetery keeper's broom propped against a tree. The man was nearby, bent over an old grave, pounding away on something with a large stone. The abandoned grave had sunk into the ground, and in the hollow there were three pups, which had recently been born. The keeper had a Latino face and a small unhesitating hand. The three pups moved awkwardly here and there, but the stone fell with a dull thud, and they could not climb out of the hollow. There was some blood, but not too much, and soon the little animals were dead. The keeper dropped the stone (it was in reality a piece of mossy headstone), took out a plastic bag and threw the animals in by the tail. He caught sight of the priest watching him and smiled humbly.

The bitch came and stood several yards away, barking. The keeper took a couple of steps towards her and she darted away, but when he turned his back she came back and continued to bark, half-heartedly. Death was there in the world, both below and above ground, chalking up its victims, no matter how small and harmless.

He was reminded of one of his first visits as a priest to a house where someone had died — a little child, during an operation. He had known the parents from church and someone had suggested that he pay them a visit. He went the same day (he had a great sense of duty back then). They had just come home from the hospital and were surprised to see him, but they let him in — perhaps unwillingly, he could not remember now; he would not have noticed if they had been reluctant, for in those days it was unthinkable to him that a priest could ever be unwelcome in a Christian house — a comfortable house with tasteless furniture and lots of silverware on display. Strange how one remembered things like that — perhaps because it had reminded him of his own parents' house. In the sitting room a boy squatted in front of a television playing a video game (he had forgotten they had another child). The woman said, 'Go to your room,' and immediately the boy abandoned his game and left. In his mind's eye the priest saw his childhood self being taught obedience by a father who shouted and a mother who hurried down the corridor in her slippers to give him a slap with what she thought was charity — it was preferable to her husband coming to the room with the belt wound a couple of turns around his hand; and the boy was not doing well at school, either. He sipped his tea and bit into a biscuit and talked about eternal life and how their other son was now in a better place, watching down on them from heaven. On the case of the video-game cartridge a soldier in armour holding a machine gun stood with his back to a large explosion. Violence was there on the floor like a bloodstain: it seemed to fit in well with the polished silverware, the china bibelots, the crocheted doilies, the talk about angels: one had to believe in hell if one were to believe in heaven. The boy had left the television on, and the soundtrack of the video game boomed in the background — perhaps it was a little gesture of defiance. After a while the woman went and turned off the television. She came back and carried on listening to the priest dutifully, nodding in agreement, saying nothing as the father smoked one cigarette after another — this had struck Father Thomas as a little rude. He had been young and healthy, and death had meant nothing to him back then, and he had had no experience of grief. His parents had still been alive at the time, and when his grandmother had passed away without pain in another town, the family had not mourned. She had lived a long, happy life — what is that old phrase? 'Full of years.' At some point he had stopped talking, but neither the man nor the woman said anything. He waited out of politeness, helping himself to another cup of tea, hoping that they would say something to which he could reply with more words of comfort — or at least they might thank him for his visit. All of a sudden he heard a low, high-pitched sound, like a dog whining, but it was the man, crying quietly while his wife looked down, saying nothing. It was unpleasant to listen to, but it would have been disrespectful to go, so he had waited patiently for it to stop, before saying a prayer and getting up to take his leave. He had tried to deny them their grief with banalities, but grief was all they had — their shelter from despair.

The sky was strewn with milky clouds. He came out to the zócalo through a side-street and made his way across the crowd of tourists and locals. There was laughter and friendly jeering and the white flash of a camera against the evening sky. Someone spoke loudly in North American English: something about the local food, how they had had better meals in the federal capital and everything was pricier than he had anticipated. Every time that a gap would open up in the crowd there would be a rush of children to fill it up. Through the large wooden door of the cathedral came a hymn sung by a congregation made up for the most part of Indians now living in the town. Father Thomas thought: how devoted they are to a faith that has helped them so little; one might as well worship a history book.

8

Milagros lay in bed staring at the thatched roof, which glistened with dew. Some women walked past outside, talking in their language — she could hear them through the thin mahogany boards: one never really got any privacy in the village. A long shadow came in through the door, and she quickly covered herself with the blanket. How strange it was that she would care about a thing like that: modesty was something one was taught in childhood, and it was hard to forget. The boy followed his own shadow into the hut, coming in as casually as entering his own home, without asking permission or saying a greeting. He held up something wrapped in cloth and said, 'This is for you, señora.'

She sat up and unwrapped her present: it was a heavy old machete. The boy waited to hear what she thought.

'Is it yours?' she asked. Her mouth felt dry, and she left it on the bed and filled a glass from the jar on the table.

'My father's, señora.'

'Did you ask him before taking it?'

The boy shook his head: no. 'He wouldn't

mind. It's an old one. It was rusty and didn't cut, but I polished and sharpened it. See how it shines?' He held its blade against a shaft of light coming through the roof of the hut. 'I made a new grip too. The wood had rotted.'

'What am I supposed — '

'You should always have one when you go to the forest, señora. For cutting — and protection.'

'I've never used a machete.' She took it in her hand again: it felt awkwardly balanced. 'Will you show me how to use it?'

The boy nodded. He asked, 'When is the father coming back?'

'Soon, I should think.'

'He couldn't save the soldier's life,' he said.

Milagros put the machete down on the bed. She said, 'The soldier needed a doctor,' and began to put on her boots.

'But Hesuklisto is more powerful than any doctor, isn't he?'

'He is. But he doesn't interfere with people's lives. Only on very rare occasions — we don't know when.'

'Has he ever helped you?'

'Me? No, he hasn't helped me,' Milagros said. She laced up her boots and glanced at the boy's bare feet. They were hard and scratched and crusted, like something one might have picked up in a refuse dump. She said, 'It's just that believing in him gives some people a certain — strength.'

'I believe in him, but I don't feel strong, señora.'

She stood up and took the machete from the bed. She said, 'Don't give up on him yet. When is your first Communion?'

'I don't know exactly. The father says soon.'

'Maybe you'll feel differently afterwards. You should talk more to Father Thomas about your questions, you know.'

'You, señora, felt differently afterwards?' the boy asked. He had an honest wish to comprehend the mysteries of the great foreign god: Hesuklisto had to be great, for his believers to have conquered the world. He knew nothing of other religions besides Christianity and the old forest gods, who seemed weak and petty and foolish to him; that much he understood.

'Oh, I don't know,' Milagros said. She saw that her reply dissatisfied him and she went on, 'I suppose I did. It's really a long time since I had my first Communion.' All she remembered about it was a white dress with a veil, and a wreath of flowers on her hair. 'You'll be making your mother proud,' she said. She rested her hand on the boy's shoulder. His collarbone stood out under his tunic and felt brittle, like something she could have unearthed from an ancient tomb. She said, 'I know she wants you to become a good Christian.'

'And you, señora,' he asked eagerly, 'are you a good Christian?'

She did not know how to reply. She said, 'Not as good as Father Thomas. I haven't been to church in a long time. Don't mind me; try to be more like him.' It made her feel uneasy to be talking about herself, even to a child. She went to the door and said, 'Shall we go?'

They went out and into the nearest trees. There was no one in the forest at that time: the men were in the fields, the women working in the village. The air was cool and humid. Milagros walked behind the barefoot boy. At a place where the path was blocked by a tangle of lianas, she raised the machete and aimed it at a branch. The woody vine was harder than she expected: the blade got stuck in it, and she had to use both her hands to get it out. The boy said with the seriousness of an instructor, 'Not like that, señora,' and took the machete from her, swung it over his head and brought it down at a slant. The blade clinked as it cut through the branch, and he gave the machete back to her with nonchalance. She tried to imitate him, hacking at the vines until he said, 'Señora,' and she stopped, panting, and saw that he was staring at her. 'Do you want to see something?' the boy said. 'It isn't far.'

'Sure.'

'You have to promise not to tell anyone.'

The woman said, a little apprehensive, 'What is it?'

'Don't be afraid, señora. There is no one around. You have to promise.'

'If it's something secret,' she said, 'why are you showing it to me?'

The boy said simply, 'I like you.'

'Is it some sort of a hideout?'

'No,' he said before disappearing into the thick undergrowth. 'Come.'

She followed him deeper into the forest, picking up her steps so as not to lose him. The machete had no sheath or shoulder strap, and it was difficult to walk carrying the heavy weight in her hand. At a steep muddy slope the boy waited to help her climb, and then he darted ahead again, calling, 'This way, señora,' and waving her on through the bushes. She followed him reluctantly, starting to regret that she had agreed to come. She caught a glimpse of him before he disappeared again — in his flowing cotton tunic he was like a little friendly ghost in a school play. After a while she heard his rough Indian voice calling her.

There was a hut in the middle of a small clearing: the traditional four mahogany walls supporting a palm roof and a door with a wooden crossbar on the outside. She guessed what it was: the god-house. She went in with slow steps, thinking that she ought to show reverence for the sacred place. The boy followed her with trepidation: he was a trespasser too; he was not old enough to join the men in worship yet. He could only guess at the use of the ceremonial utensils lying about. The clay pots and the conch and the hollowed-out trunk of a tree conjured up images of the underworld. The woman wondered why the child had brought her there. Perhaps it was a gesture of friendship — or maybe he wanted something in return. To take him along when she left the forest? He had heard men from the village talk about life in the outside world: the forest demons and the shape-shifting gods of his people were no match for the miracles of the transistor radio, the jeep and the aeroplane. She went out again. The forest was alive with birdsong. She felt a sense of comradeship, as if the boy and she were partners in crime now. The calls of the birds and the monkeys hiding in the trees kept up without a pause. The boy said, 'Now we can go. It's nearby.'

'You mean it wasn't the god-house you

wanted to show me?'

'No. Something else.'

She thought about her work. She said, 'We could come back another time. Tomorrow maybe?'

'No, señora,' the boy said. 'Now.'

'And then we'll go back?'

'Yes. I want you to see, señora. Because you are my friend.'

'Very well, very well,' she said. 'Let's go then.'

'Does Hesuklisto,' the boy said, staying put, 'only punish those who believe in him?'

'How do you mean?'

'If you only believed in the old gods, shouldn't it be they who should punish you if you did something wrong?'

Milagros listened carefully. 'I should think all gods punish in similar ways.'

The boy said, 'My father says the people who have done wrong get punished when they go to the underworld.'

'Oh, I don't think we did anything that bad,' the woman said. The boy sat with his eyes on the ground. 'The gods won't be mad at us for taking a peek, will they?'

'If you slept with one of your close relatives, the lord of the underworld will burn the thing between your legs with a hot iron,' the boy said. 'If you lied, he'll burn your mouth with it. If you stole, he'll burn your hand.'

'Have you done any of those things?'

He shook his head briskly from side to side, and his dark young face looked troubled. He went on, 'He will then boil down your soul and send you back to earth as an animal. If you did something that wasn't too bad, you'd come back as a parrot. If you were lazy, you'd turn into a dog. If you were selfish, you'd come back as a pig, and the cruel man would be a mule.'

'You're a good boy,' the woman said. 'You have nothing to worry about.'

'And do you know,' the boy said, 'do you know what the lord of the underworld will do to you if you've killed somebody, señora?' He straightened his dusty white tunic nervously. 'He will freeze your soul and boil it down until it disappears altogether.' He turned and looked at the hut in the forest with dread. 'You . . . will no longer be,' he said. The sun beamed down on them. The air smelt of the incense ash in the sacred pots of the god-house, and a monkey howled in a tree.

'What is it you want to show me?' Milagros said.

She followed him again. A short distance away he stopped and stood in silence, looking in the direction from which came the sound of flowing water. He seemed reluctant to go on: it was as if he stood at a border which he could not cross without putting himself in some sort of danger. The woman stood next to him on the edge of the stream. There was a man's body lying halfway up the sloping ground across the shallow water. 'Did you find him yourself?' she asked.

'There are more.'

'How many?'

'I've found four. Maybe there are more.'

'Are they soldiers?'

The boy denied it with a shake of his head. They crossed the stream, but did not go any closer. The boy stood there in his wet tunic, his bare feet a few inches from the water flowing noisily over the stones, watching her. He had found someone to share his secret with — perhaps it felt less terrible that way.

'I suppose,' Milagros said, 'that it happened recently.'

'Yes.'

'Did you see it happen?'

'No.'

'But you have an idea who did it,' the woman said, without apportioning blame: it did not feel right to accuse the boy who had trusted her. She waited while he threw stones in the stream and did not reply. Something in the darkness of the forest shrieked. The woman said, 'And you have no idea who they are?' The air changed direction and she caught a whiff of the rotting bodies.

'Squatters, señora,' the boy said. He stretched back his arm and slung a stone as far downstream as he could. When he ran out of stones, he gathered up another handful and hurled them one after another into the stream again, saying with feeble rage, 'They shouldn't have come to the forest.' Plop, plop — the stones fell into the water. 'You, señora,' he said, 'you understand, no? They are thieves.' He threw more stones in the stream, not horrified, but furious at the dead. 'You promised not to tell, señora, yes?' he said. 'You promise in the name of Hesuklisto?'

The woman nodded, and the boy got rid of the stones and turned to go. He was satisfied: he had shared the burden of his secret and made certain no one else would know. He said, 'Excuse me, señora,' and went bashfully into the forest to relieve himself. She stood on the edge of the water to wait for him, impatient to get back to the village. Being so close to the dead made her feel as if she were desecrating a grave. The boy had said nothing about burying them. It was difficult to believe that it was his father who had killed them, but it had to be him — he was the only Indian with a gun in those parts of the forest. The monkey in the tree began to shriek over the noise of the rushing water: an urgent, repeated rasp, sounding like a warning. She searched for the little animal with her eyes, but could not make it out in the dense foliage of the trees. When she looked down again she saw the yellow spotted pattern standing out against the muddy backdrop of the forest: a jaguar crouching on the other side of the stream some distance away, looking back at her. It seemed neither afraid nor ready to attack. It watched her a little more, then stretched its neck and lapped the water. The woman did not move: she thought that if she did, she would alarm the jaguar and make it attack. It drank noisily for a while, wiped its nose with its paw and turned its head towards her again.

A distant voice called casually, 'Señora,' and she started: the boy was looking for her. The jaguar stood up and showed its teeth, growling; the human voice had broken their truce. She had the impulse to run away — if she tried to climb up a tree, could the jaguar climb after her? She thought that at least she ought to warn the boy not to come closer, but then she feared that she might be provoking the jaguar even more. The voice enquired, still some distance away, 'Señora,' and she turned to the direction it came from, but the boy was still out of sight. When she looked back, the jaguar had stepped into the water. She said in a low voice, 'Stay where you are, Onésimo,' but he could not have heard. The animal took another step across the stream, and she prepared to defend herself. She even swore at it to psych herself up, but it made her feel ridiculous. She could never muster up the rage that was needed to hate somebody, not even an animal that might kill her. She supposed that it was a sign of cowardice — the notion that somehow one could placate an attacker by kindness. But when the jaguar crossed the water, it casually trotted away from her and into the forest. There was the noise of feet trampling through the undergrowth behind her: the boy appeared from the trees and waved.

She felt privileged that the jaguar had not attacked her — even grateful, as if killing her was its entitlement and sparing her had been an act of generosity. She said nothing to the boy about the incident because he was bound to tell the people in the village. She felt that the brief encounter between the animal and her had been like forming a pact to let each other survive. The boy said, 'We should get back, señora.'

Suddenly the monkey began to howl again: the jaguar was in the undergrowth some fifty yards away: it had come back, attracted perhaps by the boy's presence. All that stood between the animal and them was a stretch of mossy stones. When the boy saw it, he cried, 'Run, señora!' and went towards the water. His instinct was to flee. Perhaps to him this was not just a wild animal, but a god of the forest coming to punish the killings of the men lying on the hillside. There was no hope of walking carefully away from the jaguar now. Milagros had to run too. She followed the boy, splashing across the water without looking back, slipping on the rocks, trying not to fall. When she reached the other side she saw that the boy was some distance behind her: without shoes, he could not run across the water as fast as she had done. She ran back into the stream as the jaguar was entering the water on the opposite bank. In the middle of the stream the animal caught up with the boy and grabbed hold of his tunic with its teeth. He tried to escape, tugging at his tunic until the edge tore off and he fell back into the water. He stood up quickly, but the jaguar now grabbed his foot with its teeth and paw — almost playfully: the boy was an easy prey. Maybe it had an instinct for cruelty: Milagros felt betrayed. It was hard to imagine a creature without morality, guided only by an instinct for survival — the toy lion in the cot leaves an indelible mark in the mind. When she was close she raised the machete, aiming to strike the jaguar in the ribs, but it kept moving wildly and the blade just grazed its skin. Nevertheless it was enough to draw blood, and the pain made it let go of the boy and turn on her. She raised the machete again, and this time the jaguar backed off and swiped its paw at her, growling. The machete came down again and again, missing every time, but the jaguar now feared the blade that had hurt it, and after a moment it turned and ran out of the water and into the forest.

The boy was sitting in the shallow water, sobbing. His tunic was stained with blood, and more blood was gushing out of the deep cuts in his foot. The woman picked him up. He was small and light, but it was hard to carry him on the uneven ground with the machete in her other hand. She would not leave it behind: she was worried the jaguar might return. She walked as fast as she could, tripping over stones and roots, using the machete to stop herself from falling, as the boy's blood soaked her clothes and warmed her skin. She went faster than she expected past the god-house, the hills, the place where she had practised with the machete. The boy had turned silent for a while, but she did not dare stop and check on him.

In the village the women were talking among themselves and the children were running round: they all stopped and looked at her. She could not hold the child any more. She let go of the machete and put him down gently. Someone shrieked. It felt strange; she had never seen the Indians express any kind of emotion before. She was ashamed to admit that she felt almost — glad.

9

Father Thomas rode on the new mule and pulled behind the one he had borrowed from Milagros. He could tell it was not a good animal that he had been sold: it had shied at the sight of the head collar. The man who had sold it to him had refused his promise to pay the difference for a better mule when he had received the money from the diocesan office. The only good feeling he had was the relief of leaving the town. Its last houses were soon behind him: single-storeyed with brightly coloured walls whose forced cheerfulness reminded him of the laughing clown-faces one sees in a funfair. He kicked the mule gently, but it did not change its pace.

They were travelling on the side of the asphalted road. Animals scurried ahead of the passing cars, and barefoot children half-heartedly sold fruit to passing motorists; they were like school-children frogmarched to a national celebration, but instead of little paper flags they held up bags of oranges. Beside a long line of parked logging trucks a group of men were having a smoke. A colectivo packed with passengers came from the opposite direction. The man at the wheel blew his horn and raised his hand at the truck drivers without slowing down. Farther ahead the priest stopped at an army checkpoint. Two soldiers in black uniforms scrutinised his papers while a third stood behind a pile of sandbags, aiming a machine gun at him. His youth, his sullen expression, even his features reminded him of the dead lieutenant. This was how it was supposed to be, of course: obedience was incompatible with a sense of self, for a soldier as much as for a monk.

On the third day he came to the place where he had met the squatters cutting and burning trees. There was no fire, only an enormous tract of forest without any trees standing, the ground covered in soot. The animals had fled, the birds too, the air smelt of burnt wood and the ash lifted off the ground by the wind stung the eyes. Charred mahogany logs were lying about. It was expensive wood, but the squatters were smallholders, not loggers, and besides they could not sell it: there were no roads in that part of the forest that trucks could drive over. He left the vast clearing behind and entered the cool dense forest again.

Why was he going back to the village? he wondered. He would have to return to the town in a couple of months, and most of the

Indians would not miss him. Hortensia perhaps, and what about the boy? He was not sure. He felt guilty for insisting that he learned his catechism instead of joining the other children in their game. He would not be surprised if the boy was glad to hear the news . . .

He used to look forward to returning to the forest after a stay in the town, but the journey seemed too long and exhausting this time. The track, the heat, the saddle — he began to notice every inconvenience as he rode slowly towards the uplands. He tried to take his mind off his suffering: and so he was going back to England, the place where he had failed in his duty as a priest. No, he did not want to think about that now, either. He told himself: the bishop is right, of course; I have not achieved much in the forest. He had never thought of himself as a missionary, as someone whose purpose was to convert the heathen. That was an imperial view of Christianity. He did not want the Indians to give up their gods and swear allegiance to his, he just wanted to encourage them to live a life of love. Suddenly the thought crossed his mind: to give the priesthood up and stay — work as a tour guide perhaps. It was one of those ideas one comes up with more as a dare than a sincere wish.

He had done nothing else in his life; God was all there had been, as far back as he could remember, everywhere: in the sitting room and at the dining table and in the room where he slept. His father had been a priest too, an Anglican vicar in a village in the north of England. There was nothing in this forest here to remind him of his birthplace with its damp old cottages and stone pubs, the ruins of the pele tower and the fell-race; there had been a sense of security about them, or perhaps it was only childhood that made one feel that way. He had looked up to his father and it had come naturally to announce that he wanted to join the priesthood too. Then, just a year into the seminary, he had converted to Catholicism, drawn to it by its dourness, its severity, its rigour. A young man who loved absolutes — how different he had been then. His father was badly hurt by his decision, their relationship had never recovered. Every time he visited home from then on, his father made sure that he was out. His mother had to come up with some excuse: a parish meeting, a trip to the town, a doctor's appointment. He did not mind. He was too young to understand his father and feel any remorse. In fact it gave him a subtle satisfaction to be able to say that he had sacrificed his family for the Church. Well, it was all that was left to him now: he could not bring himself to abandon it.

At midday he stopped to feed and rest the mules. He had just hung the nosebags round their heads when a man in fatigues and a campesino hat came out of the trees. There were no insignia on his uniform and his rubber boots were worn and muddy. He was carrying a Sten sub-machine gun, which was very old, almost absurdly so, like something you would see behind glass in a museum. 'Coming back from the town, Father?' he said cheerfully. 'A long journey to be doing it alone.' It was as casual as if they were meeting in a busy street, two people who vaguely knew each other.

'I don't mind travelling alone,' the priest said. 'In fact I always do.'

The guerrilla rested his brash eyes on him. He said, 'You weren't travelling alone some time ago, were you?'

'No, with a friend.'

The guerrilla continued to look at him with brazen suspicion. He said, 'What happened to him, Father?'

'Oh, he's gone back.'

'An Englishman too?'

'No. Someone I met in the capital once.'

'Did he get well? I was told he was very ill.'

'A bad fever. He just needed to rest.'

'And you took him to the Indians. Well, I'm glad to hear he's fine. The forest is a dangerous place, I'm sure you know.' He turned and gave a whistle, and several armed men stepped noiselessly out of the forest. 'We'll ride with you for a while, if you don't mind,' he said.

There were about thirty guerrillas, all very young: it made them seem all the more menacing. A teenager with a gun was like a child playing with matches: one could not tell when insolence or curiosity might get the better of him. The priest said, 'I heard about the ambush.'

The man slung the Sten over his shoulder and stroked the priest's new mule. He said, 'What did you hear?'

'Soldiers. All dead.'

'Well, who knows? Maybe some got away and are hiding in the forest. We didn't come across an officer among the bodies.' His pride made him eager to talk about it. 'We keep an eye out. If we held an officer . . . '

Father Thomas said, 'Have you buried them?'

'Oh, I wouldn't bother about them, Father. Let the animals have them.'

'If you tell me where they are, I'll do it myself. They were children of God — like you.'

'Or the Devil, no?' The guerrilla grinned, then turned his back and spat on the ground: he had an instinctive respect for the man of God. When he looked at the priest again, the smile was still there on his face, wordless and hostile. He said, 'They had been on their way back to the town after having burned down some squatter settlements. They left families homeless, with nothing.'

'It's terrible.'

The man with the Sten said with a mocking expression, 'It is, isn't it, Father? But we got them this time.'

'It won't make any difference. Perhaps you even made things worse for the people you're supposed to defend.'

'Well, that's your opinion,' the guerrilla said. 'It's only a start. Now they know what we're capable of. Let them try it again. I promise you — ' The mules snorted with their noses in the bags of food and interrupted him. When he spoke again he was calmer. He said, 'The farmers don't do anyone any harm.' His men stood behind him, listening modestly to him. He said, changing his manner, 'So, you have two mules, Father.'

'One is borrowed. The other I just bought. A jaguar killed the old one.'

'You killed the jaguar?' the guerrilla said.

'No. By the time . . . I don't know whether

I should have, anyway. It has more of a right to live here than any of us.'

'Like the Indians? You think it is right to own the whole forest.'

The priest wished he could go, but the mules had not finished eating. He said, 'I don't know. Violence isn't the answer. We aren't beasts.'

'But some people are treated as if they were,' the guerrilla said.

'That is wrong, of course. But two evils don't make a right.'

'Is that all you can say? Oh, you are a priest, after all. You don't care for those poor people. You care for no one else, Father, just yourself.'

'You're probably right,' the priest said. 'It's hard to know what our motivations are. Is there such a thing as a truly unselfish act? Even charity makes you happy, proud, satisfied. I was happy living here, doing what I did. Perhaps deep inside I was expecting some sort of reciprocation — a place in heaven. Who knows?'

'Are you leaving the forest?'

'They are sending me back.'

'Somewhere you can put your skills to better use, I'm sure. A desk job? You do talk like a lawyer.'

The mules finished their food, and the

143

priest removed their nosebags. He said, 'Well, I have a long journey ahead.'

The guerrillas brought their own mules out of the trees and followed the priest in a long line up the ragged path. Their rifles clanged as the animals picked their way among the exposed tree roots and the bushes. The man with the Sten rode alongside the priest. He said, 'Your Indians have more land than they'd ever need, Father. One day they'll sell it all to the loggers and go live it up rich in the town.'

'That would be their right, of course.'

Sharp agave leaves spread across the narrow path and jabbed at the men and the animals. They passed near a cluster of houses made out of wood and iron sheets. Farther up the path a group of squatters stood waiting. When the travellers came close, the squatters took off their hats.

'Nice to see you,' the man with the Sten said. 'I apologise for being late.'

'Oh no, no. We are grateful to you, Comandante.'

The squatters looked curiously at the priest. He kicked his mule and continued down the narrow path, which cut across the trees and the lianas. He did not look back, but the silence made him assume that all eyes were on him, watching him go away. Long before the sun went down, the light had gone out under the canopy of the forest, and his inexperienced mule was reluctant to go on, so he stopped for the day. He started a fire and stoked it until it was large enough to keep the jaguar away, if it happened to be nearby. He sat by the fire and thought about going home to England. (How hard it was to be calling it home. He had tried to escape from it, but there he was going back again, without wanting to.) He had no photographs, no keepsakes, no letters from anyone — only his memories of home remained. They might as well have been a heap of ashes from a bonfire of unwanted things; he would have let the wind blow it all away if he could.

Part Three

10

They began to gather in the small church before the sun rose above the treetops. The children came first, then the men and lastly the women, having put aside the jobs in the house. A few men kept watch over the animals in the pen, in case the jaguar returned. There was always a chance of that, but a child would have been enough to raise the alarm; those men needed an excuse for not going to Mass, whose words and formalities they did not really understand. They leaned against the tall fence, tapping their machetes against their legs, watching the sun come out, saying little. In the empty village they were as bored and restless as they would have been in the church, but at least there they could smoke and chat if they so wished. The church bell stopped, the last Indians trooped into the church and a silence broken only by the occasional barking of dogs spread over the village.

At the end of the Mass they came out looking glum. They were not the sort of practised churchgoers one came across in the town: no standing outside the church exchanging pleasantries, no exuberance, no relief to have left the crowded room. The smell of incense and the image of the man on the Cross placed a burden on them every time: it was incomprehensible to them that a god would allow himself to suffer like that. Even the children were sad and speechless for a while, then the effect of the bleak ceremony went and they scattered across the village. A little girl came and sat outside the church with her back to the wall, playing with a parrot in the shade. It was tied by its foot to her arm, and she paused with some lettuce in her hand just out of reach of the bird's beak. The parrot croaked, flapped its wings and stretched its neck, but she would not let it have the lettuce.

The weather had changed. Clouds passed over the village and a weak rain fell, tapping against the dry palm roof of the church for a few minutes, leaving behind a humid air. The iron cross on the altar was not the emblem of a powerful religion; it seemed as modest and unimportant as a hand-tool or a paperweight. The priest went into the sacristy to change back into his civilian clothes. The girl outside the door still spoke to the parrot. Her voice travelled into the room, low and persistent and almost adult. The bird replied with a short croak, and the girl spoke again. She was trying to teach it to speak; in the town an Indian had once seen a man with a bird that could name things and count, and when he had come back to the village he had told everyone about it. Sometimes she lost her patience and yelled, demanding obedience. As a child, Father Thomas had resented praise and condescension, the pat on the head and the pinch of the cheek. He thought how an adult lowers his eyes to look at a child; this was how a child comes to understand God. Was not God supposed to be looking down at them all from the heavens? But he could only admire a god who lived level with the ground, humble and vulnerable and easy to ignore, enduring human ingratitude. The Indians sent him their children for confession, and they sat there trying hard to think of something — a sin. It was amusing to see their faces light up when they remembered some innocent mischief they had got themselves into, and with what glee they told him, hoping it would please him.

A man's voice sent the girl away, and there was silence. The priest assumed that the man had left too, but then he heard him coming into the church. He did not enter the sacristy: he could hear him moving among the benches in the dark. The priest called, 'Who's there?' There was no obvious reason for being afraid — he was merely curious. Through the window he could see the animals in the pen moving about slowly. The men were gone now, and a pair of boys had taken their place, each with a machete slung over his shoulder, pacing the fence earnestly.

An Indian voice said, 'Can I come in?' It sounded flat, with almost no inflection — proud; it was not asking but demanding. He guessed it belonged to Venustiano even before he came in. The Indians were small in body: if he had come across Venustiano in the dark in the town, he would have mistaken him for a child. He did not know exactly how old the Indian was. They all married very young — a boy's parents chose a wife for him when he was perhaps fifteen or sixteen, and the bride could be younger still: a childhood cut short, innocence giving its place to an inflated sense of responsibility. The room was slowly getting warm and humid. One could not hide in the shade for long: the forest sought the body out and tormented it until the sun went down, and often even at night. The Indian looked around. The silence and the heat bothered him as little as the flying cockroaches and the mosquitoes. Father Thomas thought: the human voice is deceiving; it was in one's silences that one understood another's character. It was strange to have the Indian there, in the small lonely room with the bed where he had been lying all those years — alone. There was a semblance of intimacy in the brief moment of silence. The Indian said, 'My woman is praying to your god to help the boy. Do you think she should?'

'I guess it never hurts to.'

The Indian gathered the spit in his mouth, but hesitated; perhaps he had seen how the respectable white people behaved in the town. He went to the window and spat out. From the fields in the distance came the sound of machetes chopping away; it was the second maize harvest of the year. He said, 'There are other gods here, more ancient and powerful than Hesuklisto.' Something splashed on the table: a large moth fluttered about in the bowl of water. The Indian glanced at it and turned back to the priest. 'You had a good journey, Father?' he asked coolly.

'I was in town only for a couple of days. I don't like it much there. You know how it is. You've been there yourself . . . '

'I dislike it very much,' the Indian said.

'I don't blame you. I wouldn't have gone, if it weren't for the mule.'

'Is it true you're going away?'

The moth's wings had got wet and too

heavy: there was no way they could lift it out of the water. The priest watched it circling on the water, desperately. 'I don't want to go, but have been ordered. You, at least, should be pleased about it.'

'I don't mind either way.'

'No? There will no longer be anyone to waste your people's time with stories about the foreign god,' the priest said. 'I thought you'd like that.'

The Indian said contemptuously, 'There will be another priest to take your place, I'm sure.'

'I doubt if he'd choose to live in the forest,' the priest said. He could not stand watching the moth in the water. He carried the bowl to the window and emptied it out. 'He'd probably be based in the town and come over now and then. He'd be someone who won't cause you any trouble — not like me.'

'Let's hope so.'

'Maybe you should go and talk to the bishop yourself.'

The Indian looked at him with suspicion. 'What for?'

'You could tell him how you feel about it,' the priest said. 'He'd listen to you. You are the head of the village. In fact you should've done it a long time ago. Perhaps I can arrange it.'

The Indian's expression turned hard. He

said, 'No. I'm not going to go to anyone. Let them come here.'

'That might not happen.'

'I won't go knocking on doors like a beggar. I remember how my father . . . '

'Had he been to see the bishop?'

The Indian nodded. 'He had taken me along.'

'And so?'

'He shamed himself.' He thumped on the table, as though the memory was an insect he could crush, remove from his mind for ever. 'I wish I hadn't gone. To see him bend down and kiss that ring — I can't forget that. Who was that man who could demand our obedience? My father's ancestors were kings. And the way the bishop spoke to him — me, of course, he just patted on the head. I was a little boy then, but I knew, I knew . . . My father was so proud of having been baptised. What a fool! And the bishop spoke nonsense about this and that, about God and how wonderful it was that the head of the village had joined the church at last and, if he could convince his people to join too, how Hesuklisto would be very pleased.' He spoke in an unvaried, continuous voice, hardly pausing to draw breath, letting his contempt pour out without losing his temper; he had thought long and hard about all this, and his mind was made up once and for all. 'My father believed in your god, and he said the bishop was a saint, who would protect us and our land.'

The priest said, 'I'm sorry for your father.' He thought for a moment. 'God has nothing to do with what's happening in the world.'

'Hasn't he? Then what's the point of worshipping him?' the Indian asked harshly. 'But I wasn't taken in.'

'I know that you care about your people. I wish you'd understand, even now, that I'm not the enemy.'

The Indian said, 'You are the enemy, whether you know it or not. I don't care about your good intentions.' He waited for some sort of reply, but the priest stood with the empty bowl in his hands, watching him without anger. It infuriated the Indian not to be able to get a reaction out of him. He said, 'You put my people's lives at risk. You'd say you did it out of compassion. I'd say it was arrogance.'

'You have every right to think that way. I can only imagine how it feels to be in your position. But the lieutenant is dead now. There's no danger any more.'

'No, there's no danger. And even if there is, I have my gun.'

'What can you do with it, against the

guerrillas? No, there's no reason to be afraid of them. They are ordinary people like you. Maybe you can come to an understanding.'

'I thought you were on our side.' The Indian stood in the middle of the room looking this way and that, restless. He said, 'You seem to have changed opinion recently. Perhaps you were never our true friend, were you? All you cared about was your little church — oh, and the school you are building. You haven't even finished it. What will become of it now? I don't expect the priest who'll come after you to be teaching the children.'

'I don't know,' the priest said. He put the bowl back on the table and sat down on the bed. In a few weeks he would be far away. How different England was from this place — another world. He began to count the days until his departure: five, ten, no more than twenty . . . he could not delay it more than that. And then the long flight back to London. What would it be like, going back after so long? Even his mother tongue might feel like a foreign language.

'Well, that visit with my father was the first time I went to the town,' the Indian said. 'A couple of years later I went again, alone this time. My father had gone there to sell some birds and skins, but a month had passed and he hadn't come back. My mother sent me to find him.'

'Why you, and not a grown-up from the village?'

'Out of shame, I suppose. My mother hadn't told me anything, just to go and look for him, but I suspect she had a good idea what had happened.'

'Did you find him?'

The narrow Indian face turned towards the window. 'It took me a while. I asked every Indian I came across, until I discovered him in a back street. He was drunk, his dress bloody and dirty. He had been sleeping rough. He had no money left. Everything he'd made in the market he'd given to buy wine.' He went up to the window as if he had seen something outside, but just stood there with a glazed expression. His constant fury had drained out of him, and all that was left was helplessness. 'I suppose this is what you call a confession, Father?' he said mockingly, turning to face the priest.

'No,' the priest said. 'You go to confession to admit to having done something wrong.' He looked at the young man questioningly: hesitation glimmered in the Indian's eyes. He could tell. An interrogator relies on the face as much as a lover does: a little sidelong glance, the tongue passing over the lips, the cheeks tingling with shame or fear. He said, 'But you haven't done anything wrong, have you?'

Indecision vanished in a flash from the dark Indian eyes and the other man said, 'No, I've done nothing wrong.'

'Did you come to tell me that?'

The Indian said with the bitter candour of a man forced to admit something, 'The woman wants you to come and see the boy.'

'Oh, of course.'

'And to pray for him.'

They went out. Someone was coming down the hill from Venustiano's house, slowly, carrying a bag and machete over his shoulder. He greeted the two men with an unsmiling face and a slow raise of his hand. The priest said, 'How's the boy, Ernesto?'

'Asleep.'

'Will he be fine?'

'He may have a limp. Who knows?' He was wary about giving information freely. He knew things that were hidden from the rest of his people — truth was to be found in the shadows: perhaps he thought of himself as a shaman. Venustiano did not speak.

The priest said, 'Does he need any medicines?'

'I gave him medicines,' the old Indian said and went away. His tunic fell heavily over his

159

shoulders and it swayed with each step. Frayed and dirty, it was like the flag of a retreating army, flying with wounded pride. He had sewn a small breast-pocket in it to carry his glasses. He never wore them in public; vanity was as much at home in the forest as anywhere else. The dogs of the village herded round him as he walked on in his dirty white tunic, barefoot, carrying over his shoulder the bag that contained his healing powers. The sun was high and the air was warming up and he was late for going to his plot. The priest and Venustiano went in the opposite direction. A dog appeared on the top of the hill and began to bark, but when they came up to it, it walked timidly away, stealing glances at them. A voice came from inside the house, 'Is that you, Father?' and a face with a flicker of a smile showed at the door. Venustiano turned round and went away without a word: he did not want to be part of the ritual. The priest said in a low voice, 'How is the boy, Hortensia?'

'Oh, not well, Father.' She glanced at him with intense eyes and turned away, saying shyly, as if to herself, 'God bless you for coming.' He admired her maturity despite how young she was: she must have given birth as soon as she had entered puberty. She wore her long black hair in a single braid, which she had decorated with toucan feathers. A necklace of plastic beads hung from her neck. He followed her into the house. She said, 'He hasn't slept much. He had a bad dream about the jaguar. He's afraid of going to sleep again.'

Onésimo was lying under a blanket. His eyes darted from his mother to the visitor. Father Thomas bent down and touched the boy's forehead. He said, 'The peace of the Lord be with you always.'

'And also with you,' the Indian woman said. The priest blessed the boy, and the Indian woman said, 'His father promised him to kill the jaguar.'

'It could well be hundreds of miles away by now,' the priest said.

'He'll find it.'

'He'd be wasting his time. And risking his life.'

Onésimo settled back on the petate and gazed calmly at the priest, now that the blessing was over. The dog put its head through the door, but the woman sent it away.

'Thank God the kind lady was with him,' the woman said.

'Yes. Milagros saved the boy's life.'

'My husband is very angry, Father.'

'At the jaguar?'

161

'At the squatters. They burn down the forest, and the jaguar has to come to the village to find food.'

The priest sat on the earthen floor in the small, dark room watching the boy as the noonday sun burned outside. He was like a prophet who knew the world would end but could not bring himself to tell his followers the truth.

★   ★   ★

Hortensia slept on the floor with her back against the wall and a stack of yellowed fotonovelas on her lap. She had been looking at the photographs, trying to guess the plot of the story: she could not read. Perhaps it was better that way; she made up a new plot every time that she picked up a magazine. The man put another stick on the fire that was burning in the middle of the small house and knelt next to the mat where the boy lay awake with the dog curled up at his feet. Ever since the jaguar attack the boy had been afraid of the dark.

'It'll keep burning all night,' the Indian told the boy. His rifle was beside him on the mat. He picked it up and began to clean it. 'Now go to sleep,' he said. 'I'll stay up.'

'I can't,' the boy said firmly, as if he had

been asked to do something impossible.

'The jaguar won't come here,' the man said. The barrel of the rifle glinted in the glow of the fire as he rubbed it with the rag, and the smell of lubricant spread across the room. The boy watched from under the covers. 'But I wish it would,' the man added, 'so that I'd have the chance to kill it.' The light of the fire stretched just as far as the door. Beyond, it was completely dark. He was secretly worried too — not about the animal. If one believed in the ancient gods one ought to believe in dreams too, and he knew that to dream of a jaguar meant that strangers would come: he wondered who they might be. He continued to clean the rifle. The boy moved his feet, and the dog woke up and looked round, then snuggled down again. The Indian said, 'A man's soul can't make it to the underworld without the help of the soul of his hunting dog.'

The boy looked at him wearily. Venustiano knew that look: the boy was not interested in his stories. It saddened him to think that the old religion might die with him, but he was young and there was still plenty of time to teach the children and those children's children about it. Some would learn — unless the foreign father had already convinced them that the gods of the forest did not exist.

He went on, 'You see, after a man dies his soul goes on a journey which brings him to a river full of crocodiles. If he has been good to his dog when he was alive, the dog's soul will carry him across. But if he has been mean to it, it won't help him. This is why one shouldn't be mean to his dog.'

The boy said nothing, and he continued, 'The crocodiles aren't real, of course. They are illusions, but the man's soul doesn't know that. The river is made of the tears of the people who wept for him when he died — his wives, his friends and his children.' He gave the boy a sidelong glance.

'What is on the other side?' the boy asked.

'The forests of the underworld.' The Indian removed the bolt from the rifle to clean it too.

'And there the journey ends? In the underworld?'

'Well,' the Indian said, 'sometimes. Or the soul might ascend to one of the five heavens.' He picked up the oil can and said, 'It depends on the kind of person he was, and the way that he died.'

He was pleased to hear the boy asking questions for once. He left the story unfinished, waiting for him to ask about it, but the eyes under the blanket watched him dully.

He said, 'Let me tell you how the gods

created people. Do you want to know? They tried three times before they succeeded.' He put down the rifle and scratched the floor. 'First they made men out of mud, but they melted when they sat by their fires and when it rained.'

Something in the story had caught the boy's imagination. He said, 'That's what Hesuklisto's father did too.'

The man frowned. 'Is that so?'

'He made the first man from mud. The father says that then God cut a part off the man's body and made the first woman with it.'

'Ah, the father knows only part of the story,' the Indian said dismissively. 'The men of mud did not last.'

'The father says we all come from them. They married and had children, and their children had children and — '

The Indian said, 'Well, the father is wrong.'

'Wrong?' the boy said. He crossed his arms under the blanket and stretched his legs, waking the dog again. 'The father says . . . ' He knew the story of Creation well; the foreign father had not mentioned anything about any other kind of people apart from the first man of mud and his wife.

'You pay too much attention to him,' the man said, and looked at his son with a hint of despair. 'Do you want to know the truth or not?'

'The father has read many books . . . '

'Books don't tell the truth. How could they? It's foreigners who write them, and they've never been here.'

'How do you know your story is true?'

'Because my grandfather told it to me. And he hadn't read it. He had been told it by his own grandfather.'

He remembered his grandfather again, and how he used to sit with him and listen to his stories while his father lay on his petate drinking from a bottle. He said, 'I'm telling you so that when I die and you get to be head of this village, you'll tell them to your children and our people's children. That way our stories won't be forgotten.'

'I don't want to be head of the village. I want to go and live in the town.'

The man picked up the rag he used to clean the gun and squeezed it until his fingers dripped with oil. He had taken the boy along to the town once. He had wanted him to see how unhappy and cold and friendless the people were over there, but instead the boy had been fascinated by the music and the cars and the shops that served hot food. The Indian wished he had not done it. He said, 'They will treat you like an animal there. Your home is here.' He looked at the boy; he had turned his face to the wall. 'You will be a beggar,' the man said with feeble rage.

'Can't Mother have another boy? You could make him leader instead.'

'You are my firstborn. It's you who should take over. It's your right — and responsibility.'

Neither spoke for a short while, then the boy muttered, 'What sort of men . . . '

A feeling of great love came over Venustiano: if only the boy could understand how much he loved him. He picked up the rifle again and said, 'Well, after the men of mud came the men of wood. They didn't look much different from us, but they had neither a heart nor a soul. They could do almost everything that we can do — hunt, work the fields, build houses, cook. But they didn't kneel to the gods, pray or hold ceremonies to honour them.'

The boy took his arms out of the blanket and began to push the dog off him, but then stopped, as if he had remembered his father's story about the river of the underworld and the soul of a man's dog. He asked dutifully, 'Were the men of wood like the foreigners?'

The man nodded. 'They had children and spread across the earth, wandering about because they were unhappy. Their faces never showed any other emotion, their skin was dry and yellow, and they mistreated their animals.'

On the other side of the room the woman slept quietly. The Indian finished cleaning his rifle and wrapped it in an old linen cloth. Shadows from the flickering flames played about the walls as he stood and hung the wrapped-up rifle on the wall. When he passed in front of the fire, his small wiry frame showed through his tunic like a puppet in a shadow play; the boy could not imagine him killing the great jaguar. He sat back down next to the boy and said, 'So the gods were very disappointed with the men of wood and decided to destroy them. They made rain to fall day and night, and ordered the animals to kill them. The jaguars and the eagles and even their own dogs attacked them and tore most of them to pieces.'

'Not all of them?'

'Those who survived turned into the monkeys who live in the forest.'

The boy was thoughtful for a moment. He said, 'I feel sorry for them. I don't think it was their fault. After all it was the gods who made them, no?'

'Yes. But the gods allowed men to do what they wanted, and the men chose to be bad.'

'This is not very different from what the father tells us in church. Hesuklisto let the people do what they wanted, and they did wrong too. But he didn't destroy them. He loves people and waits for them to understand their mistake and change their ways.'

'Change their ways, eh? Hesuklisto will be waiting for ever. The foreigners will always be bad.'

'The father says . . . '

'The father, the father . . . You pay too much attention to that man. Remember he isn't one of us.'

The Indian felt tired. He had worked all day in the field, cutting maize and stacking it up to dry. If the boy had not been ill he would have helped him, but this time he had had to do it alone. He lay down on the earthen floor and stretched out. The boy asked worriedly, 'You won't go to sleep, will you?' and the man answered, as love welled up in his heart, 'No, no, I'm just resting my back for a moment.' The boy lay back and covered himself with the blanket, staring at his father.

'When the gods decided to create another kind of man,' the Indian went on, folding his hands behind his head, 'they ordered the jaguar, the coyote, the parrot and the crow to bring them the maize of the fields of heaven. With that maize they made the flesh and blood of the new man.' He lay on the hard

169

earthen floor; the petate where he slept with his wife was a few feet away, but he did not mind. He was a hunter and he slept in the forest sometimes, if he tracked an animal far away from the village. The boy was quiet. The Indian said, 'The men of maize were our forefathers. They were very intelligent and could predict the future. They honoured the gods whom they could see in the forest.' He was glad the boy was listening now. He had tried so many times to tell him some of the ancient stories, but he hadn't been interested until now. The dog lifted and dropped its tail a couple of times to shoo some insect away. 'The gods were pleased with the men of maize at first, but slowly began to fear their intelligence and ability to tell the future. They were afraid they might challenge their power one day. So they burned the people's eyes so that they could no longer see the gods. The only time we people can catch a glimpse of the gods is during the ceremonies in the god-house.' The Indian tried to imagine how life would be if he could see the gods. He would have spoken to them and asked them to help him keep his ancestors' land. He said, 'Do you want to hear another story?'

The boy did not reply. The Indian turned and looked at him: he had fallen asleep. The man wondered how much of what he had said the boy had heard after all. The fire in the middle of the house was dying out. He threw another stick on the glowing embers and listened to it crackle as it caught fire. Sparks flew up into the air and died out. He stared at the boy, thinking how fortunate he was. If he did not have him, he would have left nothing behind when he died; it would have been as if he had never existed.

11

Venustiano waded across the shallow stream with bare feet. It was pleasant to feel the cold water on his skin. He thought with scorn of those who wore shoes: he did not need them himself — and he was convinced that they would be slowing him down in the mud and water. Oh, let the foreigners wear their boots and trousers, he thought. It was a privilege for one's bare feet to touch the earth. One day he would be a feeble old man, unable to walk ... He thought with dread of the time when he would be spending his days on a petate. He came to the other side of the stream and walked along the edge of the water, first upstream, then downstream, looking for signs that the jaguar had been there to dig for turtles in the mud. With his intent, searching stare and careful steps he seemed like something other than just a hunter with a machete and rifle: he was not unlike a predator. After going some distance in either direction without coming across any tracks, he came back to the place where he had first crossed the stream and followed the path into the forest. Not long ago he had been through there, but the razor-sharp ferns had already grown across it again and he had to clear his way with the machete, pausing to check for scratch marks on the trees. It was the way one jaguar let another know it was around — but did it have to? He wondered whether an animal would abandon a habit, the way that people did when it made no sense any more; the jaguar was probably the last one in these parts of the forest. No one had seen one in a very long time before it had come.

He had never hunted a jaguar — or even seen one, for that matter. In his grandfather's days there had still been many. He remembered his grandfather telling him how the ancient kings wore their pelts as a symbol of their authority, and how the great soldiers and hunters decorated their clothes with jaguar teeth and claws. Venustiano was a leader too — in the old days he would have been a king. The path widened and he did not need the machete any more. The trees were larger here and shrouded in vines, mahogany and cedar with large exposed roots and dense-leafed branches. He lifted the rifle and squinted at a shadow in the undergrowth some distance away, but it was only a bush in the dim light. For a long time afterwards his heart beat fast at the mistaken belief that he had found the animal.

He had not used the rifle since the day he had shot the squatters. After he had found the lieutenant dead, he had gone over and looked at them closely. They lay in the mud with open eyes. He felt no satisfaction that he had not missed a shot — only relief. He had had no bullets left. If anyone had still been alive he would have had to use his machete . . . It was better not to think about it. He had done his duty to his people as their leader. Why had he told no one, then? An appalling feeling of guilt came over him, surprising him. He tried to convince himself that what he had done was not that terrible: the dead were Christians, and the foreign father said that when people died they joined Hesuklisto in heaven. Holding the rifle with a clammy hand, he walked on, a small human figure in a worn white tunic standing out in the half-light.

At midday he came to a small lily-pad lake edged with reeds where he stopped to rest. He did not come out of the trees straight away, but stayed hidden for a while and listened: there was only the birdsong and the buzz of insects. He scanned the shores of the lake in case the jaguar had come to drink, and came out and sat on a rock on the edge of the water, putting the rifle and machete down next to him. He ate the food the woman had prepared for him and continued to watch the lake. He had set off from the village before dawn and even though he was not particularly tired, he was very hungry. He felt the warmth of the rock in his body, and he turned his face to the sky: one day the sun god would come down and put an end to the world. He remembered how the foreign father had brought another priest to the village once, and Venustiano had talked to him about their gods. The priest had smiled and patted him on the shoulder. How he hated to be treated like a child . . . Perhaps the foreigners knew many things, but they did not know anything about the forest. They would not survive long if they came to live in the forest — live, that is, like he and his people did, in small wooden houses without electricity or running water. When the foreigners did come to live in the forest, he thought, they opened roads, cut down the trees and built houses just like those in their towns.

He heard a short dry sound, like a twig breaking underfoot. He quietly picked up the rifle and turned round. The trees began a few yards away. He bolted the gun and held it at his waist, ready to fire, while his eyes moved across the trees. A bird sat on a branch, pecking at a fruit; he tried to ignore the noise and listen for other sounds. He stayed like that for several minutes, waiting for something to happen, but nothing moved in the darkness among the trees. He should not be wasting any more time. He stood up and slung the rifle over his shoulder — then he heard the crack of twigs again. He quickly unslung the rifle and turned it in the direction of the sound, but then hesitated; he could not bring himself to shoot at something when he did not know what it was.

He did not hear the sound again. When he went to investigate, he could tell from the marks in the undergrowth that a heavy animal had been through there. He could not imagine that a jaguar would be that heavy. It could have been something else — a tapir perhaps. He regretted not having fired: he would have liked to return to the village with a big kill like that. He followed the animal's tracks, which soon petered out, but he did not abandon his search until the evening. Then he killed a toucan and roasted it, keeping its feathers for the woman. He lay to sleep on the ground. There were no clouds — he could see the sky clearly wherever he turned. It had been a night like this, he remembered, when his grandfather had woken him up to show him the stars. He had pointed them out and talked about the moon goddess and the god of the blood-red star, who moves in the sky and gives people eye diseases. The god of the great star, on the other hand, is lazy and lies in his hammock all day while his younger brother, the sun, goes hunting. The Indian kept his eyes fixed on the dark infinite space, with the rifle resting heavily on him. An ordinary man could make no difference in the world . . . If he had been his grandfather's true descendant things might have been different: the right sort of blood — wise and brave and patient — would have flowed inside him. But the line of royal blood had been broken, and he was no better than any man in the village — perhaps he was worse: half of a foreigner. He tried to think what else he might have done to protect their land from the squatters, but no idea came to his mind. He was not wise, not even a little clever; he did not deserve to be a leader.

In the morning he began his return journey via a different route. It was nearly impossible to hunt a jaguar without a trained dog. If he could spare a few more days perhaps — but he had promised the woman that he would return: the maize was unharvested and the boy was still not well enough. How he disliked being a farmer . . . The sky was overcast and the grass was wet from the moisture of the night. He still kept his eye out for any signs that the jaguar was about, cradling the rifle in the crook of his left arm and holding the machete with the other. His feet were numb with cold from the dew on the grass, but it pleased him to tell himself that he could stand it. He sought adversity in order to overcome it; it had been like that since he had been told as a boy that he was descended from royalty. A sense of duty — to his ancestors, to his people — was never far from his thoughts. He had tried to prepare himself for his future role as leader by going without food or water for days, swimming in cold water, holding his hand over a lit candle until the pain brought tears to his eyes. It was an education — a secret he had not shared with anyone, not even with his grandfather who had told him about the old kings. Venustiano had thought he had been ready when the time had come to become head of the village, but now he believed that he would never be good enough. He walked on, deep in thought, forgetting for a moment his mission.

He saw something move out of the corner of his eye, and he dropped the machete and turned towards it at once, taking the rifle in both hands. There was a shadow in the undergrowth, and it seemed to him that it was moving. This time he did not hesitate. He raised the gun, took aim and fired. He bolted the rifle again. His hands shook as he walked forward, keeping the rifle raised and his finger on the trigger. There was a splash of blood in the grass. He kept going in the direction in which the animal ought to have fled. The forest was quiet now. There was no birdsong or monkeys howling, and he unwillingly listened to his own heavy breathing and the sound of his feet brushing against the grass. He had never felt afraid like that before, afraid of death, of the possibility that he was going to die violently so young. Until then death had been something like his grandfather's fables: something that would happen somewhere far away in time and place, something painless like a dream. The killing of the squatters came to his mind again; had they felt any pain before they had died? He went deeper into the forest, holding the rifle with clammy hands as the shadows of the trees seemed to close in on him. He felt like talking — anything, just to break the silence, but he told himself that he had to keep quiet.

There was a flash of yellow colour somewhere to the side of him, but his first thought was that he was mistaken because he heard nothing. Then he turned his head and saw the jaguar jumping out of the undergrowth and

179

coming at him fast. He fired without taking aim. The bullet struck the animal in one of the hind legs, and it stumbled, which just gave the man time to bolt the rifle before the jaguar resumed its attack. The second bullet hit it in the shoulder as it pounced. It had jumped with such force that the Indian had to run backwards to avoid being knocked down, and it fell heavily on the grass. It roared, tried to get up, but could not. As it lay on its side, the Indian noticed the long deep cut on its side from the white woman's machete. He bolted the rifle again and took careful aim at the jaguar's head. The animal stopped trying to stand and watched him with unblinking eyes, breathing noisily with its speckled chest moving up and down. The Indian fired. Then, as the sound died down, he felt as if he were completely alone in the silent forest, in the whole world.

Part Four

12

'Bless me, Father, for I have sinned.'

The Indian woman knelt on the other side of the beaded curtain and crossed herself. There was no confessional in the church: in order to hear a confession, Father Thomas would hang a beaded curtain over the door to the sacristy, with the penitent and him standing on either side of it. He looked at the woman through the beads. She had rested her forehead on her clasped hands and bowed with eyes shut, a small young woman dressed in a tunic sewn with coloured ribbons. She was like a statue symbolising piety, humble and innocent, unlike anyone he had ever come across. He waited, but the woman hesitated — she looked up and quickly looked down again; perhaps she had forgotten what she had to say next. The priest said, 'Don't you want a chair, Hortensia?'

'Oh no, Father.'

He helped her with the words of the sacrament. 'How long has it been since your last confession?'

'It was before you went to the town to buy the mule, Father.'

'And of what sins do you accuse yourself?'

The woman said without raising her head, 'Isn't it a sin to lie, Father?'

'Yes, of sorts. I suppose . . . '

'Oh, Father,' the kneeling woman said. 'I regret what I did very much.'

'Can't you regret it seated?'

The woman shook her head from behind the curtain. 'No, no, Father,' she said. 'I must stay like this.'

The plastic beads sparkled in the sun coming through the window. He stifled a yawn: he was tired. Ever since his trip to the town he had fallen into a state of inertness, as if he had contracted some silent tropical disease that had no easy cure. He listened to the children playing noisily somewhere in the village and wondered whether any of them would remember him in a year's time. He was, he thought with self-mockery, the sort of man who at his deathbed expected tears and the lives of those whom he was leaving behind never to be the same — what a consolation it must have been to the Hindu man of the past to know that his wife would burn alive with his body in the same fire. He ought not to be vain; another priest would take his place and he would be forgotten.

Hortensia was the only person in the village whom he could claim to have sincerely converted, even though he did not think he had tried. He was not certain what had attracted her to the Christian faith. He remembered, with wry amusement aimed at his vanity, how Milagros had told him once that the Indian woman was in love with him.

He looked down at her with affection. 'Very well,' he said. 'Please tell me what you lied about.' He assumed it would be nothing important. He stared at her as she knelt hunched over the earthen floor, and he regretted having given her his religion, as if he had passed on a contagion. Belief in Christ ought to be an invitation to joy, and not to constant guilt and fear and begging for mercy. God was not a dictator. Religious practice was supposed to encourage humility, but so often it only gave one a sense of worthlessness. 'Being here,' he said, 'means you are sincerely remorseful.'

'I lied about the cow,' the woman said, pressing her clasped hands against her forehead, keeping her eyes shut.

'Please explain.'

'I told everyone,' the woman said, 'that I bought it in the town.'

'Are you talking about the cow that you bought to replace the one killed by the jaguar?'

She nodded. Her black hair was parted in

the middle and tied up firmly at the back. 'It was my idea, Father. Don't blame my husband. We couldn't have bought the cow otherwise. I paid ten thousand for it, half what they'd ask in the town. It was all our savings. The jaguar took it away.' She said, 'Is it a sin to be pleased that it's dead?'

'Well, in some ways. Don't worry. God understands your reasons.'

'I'm very proud of my husband for killing the jaguar. Have you seen its skin, father? He'll sell it in the town. He says it would've brought in even more if it didn't have the machete cut. It'll still be a lot of money, though.'

The priest said, 'I'm sure your husband knows it's illegal to trade in jaguar skins these days. He might end up in prison.'

'He knows it, Father.'

'If the police catch him, the boy and you will be left alone. Who would work the land then?'

'Those people in the town won't tell the police.'

'I didn't know your husband had friends there.'

'Oh no, they aren't his friends, Father. He sells them the birds that he traps now and then.'

'Is this where the ten thousand for the cow

came from? From selling live birds?'

The woman said, 'He only does it once or twice a year, Father.'

He disapproved but did not have the right to accuse the Indians; the forest, which was supposed to belong to them by law, would not miss a few parrots. 'Your husband doesn't seem to be very proud to have killed the jaguar himself,' he said. 'I would've thought he'd be pleased to have rid the village of the danger. And after what happened to the boy.'

'Oh, he doesn't want to talk about it.'

The priest remembered when the jaguar had killed his old mule, and the fear that was haunting him ever since; perhaps the Indian felt something similar. 'Well, you haven't come to talk about him, have you?'

The question confused the woman. 'Him? I came ... '

'To tell me about the lie.'

'Yes, yes. I know I have sinned, Father.'

'That's good. Like I said, I accept your remorse. You are a good person, Hortensia. It's impossible not to make mistakes in our lives. Under the circumstances ... a little lie like that ... Well, it's not that important.' He could not think of something better to say — it was as if he had forgotten the stock phrases one gets to learn as a priest. He looked with admiration at the meek Indian woman behind the beaded strings. 'Don't worry too much about it,' he said.

The woman mumbled, 'I don't understand, Father.' Her voice faded away, and she turned and checked the front door to see whether anyone was coming. When she turned back she said, 'Isn't lying wrong? You tell us so yourself.'

The priest said, 'Yes, of course.' What could he tell her? He asked, 'Who did you buy the cow from?'

He assumed that she had gone to one of the other Indian villages, but the woman shook her head. She said, 'From the squatters.'

'Was it your husband's idea?'

'Oh no, no,' she said briskly, as if to deny a very grave accusation. 'It was mine, Father. We needed another cow. There was no other way. And he couldn't go there himself. He's very proud.'

'I would've gone with you, if you had asked me. Wasn't it unsafe for you to go?'

'No, I am a woman. I don't answer back. And I know how to bargain.'

'You are a good person.'

He could tell that his praise embarrassed her even though she did not appear to blush. Someone else might think the Indians did not feel shame or shyness or modesty, but he had lived with them long enough to know otherwise.

'I did what had to be done,' she said. 'They said they didn't want to sell me the cow for so little at first. It was an old cow. But I could tell they were just trying to haggle. Those people think us fools.'

A flash of innocent pride lit her eyes: it was a relief to have a little sense of self-worth, whatever one accused oneself of. Then her mood changed again and she pleaded, 'I am sorry for the lie. Do you believe me, Father?' stretching her hand through the curtain.

'I do. Well, say five Our Fathers for your penance.'

'Yes, Father.' She knelt on the floor, small and shy and shaking with — hopelessness perhaps. She looked lost in the crude church with the earthen floor and the badly made benches, like a beggar coming to the door of what turns out to be a poor household. He had granted her forgiveness, but he had the impression that it was not enough for her. Perhaps she expected to suffer genuinely for her unimportant sin: the image of the bloodied Christ on the Cross was engraved on a pious mind. As she began to mumble the words of her penance, her sincere remorse was replaced by a mechanical recitation, which was hardly comprehensible. He pulled his chair closer to the curtain and leaned forward, trying to listen. A smell of mingled hair ointment and body odour passed through the strings of beads, and the fear of intimacy forced him to sit back in his chair. He waited for the woman to finish. When she completed her penance, she added in a hesitant voice, 'There's something else, Father.' She bent lower, her hands clasped together, until her elbows touched the floor, and stayed there. Someone went slowly past outside, balancing a large bundle of maize on his head. For a brief moment his shadow fell like a prying stare over the room that was the church.

'Another sin, Hortensia?' the priest said kindly. 'Very well. Tell me about it.'

'The boy, Father.'

'He did something wrong?'

The young woman said unexpectedly, 'Father, did Hesuklisto hurt the child?'

'Why do you say that? Jesus loves us all, even the worst sinner. He doesn't punish anyone.'

'The boy insists that Hesuklisto sent us the jaguar, Father.'

'Why would God do that?'

She leaned forward with dread, as if bowing to a statue. 'To take revenge for the dead.'

'What dead?' the priest said.

'The boy found them in the forest.'

'Where?'

'Near the god-house.'

The priest stood up and moved the curtain aside. 'Better come in,' he said. The woman was surprised, but obeyed — she probably assumed that kneeling in front of the curtain was not enough when the sin was so great. She had never been in that room. The narrow camp bed, the table, the clerical vestments in the open wardrobe, the cross on the wall were as awe-inspiring as anything she might have seen in the god-house, if she were allowed in. She sat hesitantly on the edge of the bed. The priest asked, 'Was that where the jaguar attacked him?'

'Yes. There are four dead.'

'All men?'

She nodded. 'The boy says they're squatters.'

She stared at him with fear in her dark innocent face. It was not him she was afraid of, but the God he spoke for. She was one of the few people in the village who listened to the gospel readings, and she understood them literally: the death of the firstborn in Egypt and the destruction of Sodom and the plagues that God had visited on sinners. Unexpectedly she kissed his hand — he had never liked that old habit. He pulled his hand away, embarrassed, then saw the expression on her face and regretted making her think that he had rejected her remorse. He said in a calm voice, 'The boy has an idea who did it, I guess. Did he tell you?'

'They were shot, Father,' the woman said. She did not have to say more; he understood: it was unlikely that anyone other than Venustiano could have done it. Still he wanted to be sure. Why had the boy told her? Secrecy was a disease; it was not long after becoming a priest that he had made that observation. The way the mind fights the knowledge of a secret struck him as similar to the manner in which the body tries to rid itself of a tumour. One feels impelled to share what one knows, and suffers when forced to keep it hidden; perhaps sharing knowledge was a primal urge. A certain look, a slight movement, a blush creeping up the face betrayed something intended to remain secret. A medieval inquisitor would try to extract it with tools and procedures rather like surgery. He thought: the heretic's fork, the iron maiden, the rack, the thumbscrews may seem crude today, but at the time they were the equivalent of the truth-serum and the polygraph.

The Indian woman sat on the edge of the bed with her head bowed and her hands clasped on her lap. There was a small rosary between her fingers. He had not noticed it until then. Blood drained from her fingers as she clasped it tightly: it was like a snake that had wrapped its coils around its little helpless victim. She said, 'He's a good man . . . '

The priest asked harshly, 'You know why he did it? Or why he hasn't buried them? There is a chance that . . . The guerrillas aren't far from here.' It was unfair to frighten the woman about it — it must have taken a lot of courage to tell him. 'Have you talked to your husband about it?' he said.

'No, Father.'

'You did the right thing by telling me, Hortensia. I'll make sure . . . '

'Hesuklisto shouldn't have punished the child, Father. He's done nothing wrong.'

'I'm sure God has nothing to do with it,' the priest said.

'If you say so,' the woman said without conviction, twisting the rosary round her fingers.

'Do you remember the act of contrition?'

'Yes, Father.' She got down on her knees and bowed her head again, folding her hands in prayer.

He felt pity — but also proud of her, as if she were a child he had raised to be good. He wondered how the priest who would take over from him would treat her. He tried to imagine him: someone young, perhaps straight from the seminary; the forest was not a sought-after post. The Indian woman finished the act of contrition, and the words of absolution came out of his mouth mechanically: 'God, the father of mercies . . . ' She tried to repeat them too, but he silenced her with a pressing of his finger to his lips and continued. He thought how easy it was to die. Death asked for so little in return for eternal nothingness: a bullet in the temple, a cut in an artery, a few drops of poison on the lips — and a little patience. It was life that demanded a great constant effort. He finished the confession and walked with the woman to the door, keeping his hands firmly in his pockets in case she attempted to kiss them again. She went out into the street and walked under the hot afternoon sun up the hill towards her house. He watched her, and his thoughts felt like blood spurting out from a wound. He knew there was no loving or merciful God, but sometimes he still yearned for that little comfort of doubt.

13

Venustiano pulled another ear of maize from its dry stalk, peeled off the husks and threw it in the basket. It was December: he was late with the harvest, but the days were still dry and hot, and he only had a small crop — in a couple more days he would finish with it. The stalks were taller than him, and his frayed straw hat disappeared among them as he picked up the basket and moved across the maize field, working in an ordered, careful way. A few birds hiding in the crops flew off as he brushed against the dry leaves. He paused to wipe the sweat from his forehead and watched their flight with tired eyes.

He was alone. His land was some distance from the other families' land in the village. Like them he had three separate plots, which he planted in rotation — maize for two years, then onions and potatoes, before completely abandoning the plot to recover. He would plant his second piece of land for the next three years and after that the third. That was the way to farm, and not the way that the squatters did it, by exhausting the land until it was totally barren. Then they cleared another large part of forest and did the same thing again; one day, not too far in the future, there would be no more trees and the soil would only be good for grass to feed the cattle. Then the squatters would starve and, with them, his people too. A gentle wind rippled the top of the maize and shook the trees in the distance where the forest began. He went back to work. He would normally carry his machete on him, but there was no reason for it now: the jaguar was dead. When his basket was full, he walked out of the field and emptied it onto the pile of ears of maize drying in the sun.

At home he spread the straw mat out on the floor and sat down next to a heap of already dried maize ears. He picked up a pair and rubbed them against each other until no more grains fell onto the mat, then pressed out the last grains on the cobs with his thumbs, threw the cobs away and picked up another pair of ears. In a corner of the room the boy was studying the jaguar skin. The Indian said, without looking up from his task, 'Put that away. It is bad enough as it is. You might stretch the tear.'

The boy folded the skin, wrapped it with a cloth and tied it with a string. When the man had brought the skin back from the hunt, the woman had scraped the flesh from the inside,

196

nailed the skin to a frame, stretching it taut, and coated it with salt. She had kept it out in the sun, adding more salt every day, until the skin was completely dry. The man would sell it the next time he went to the town. He glanced at the boy who was sitting on the floor, scratching the earth idly.

'Don't just sit there,' he said. 'There's work to be done.'

'We should check the head,' the boy said. 'Just in case. Mother said it'll fetch as much as the skin.' He looked at his father, waiting for an answer.

The man said with his back to the boy, 'It won't. There's a big hole in it.'

'Did you have to shoot it in the head?' the boy asked. He wanted to know everything about the jaguar hunt. He had asked before, and what little he had learned he turned over in his mind constantly: the animal stalking his father and the attack, and how he had shot it without taking aim. The boy had taken out the bullet lodged in its skull with a knife and kept the crushed piece of metal in a pouch round his neck like a talisman.

'Yes,' the man said. 'Now come and sit down.' He continued with his work. The boy watched him, but the Indian did not look up. There was a look of awe in the boy's face: he had never looked at him like that before. It was something that he had been wishing for for a long time, his son's admiration, but now that he had earned it, it did not please him. He said, 'Give me a hand.'

'Can I have a look first?'

Venustiano threw away a pair of empty cobs, picked up two more ears of maize and began to rub them together.

The boy watched with hesitation. He said, 'I'll have a quick look. Then I'll come and help you.'

'Go and get the alcohol first,' the man said. He stole a glance at the boy and a feeling of affection burned inside him. 'Be careful.' He finished shelling the pair of maize ears and gathered together the grains that were scattered around the mat as the boy hobbled out of the door. The Indian watched him furtively, wondering whether the boy would ever walk properly again.

On a shelf fixed to one of the poles of the roof was a large clay jar. When the boy came back with the alcohol, he carefully placed the jar on the floor and lifted the jaguar's head out. He looked at it with wonder. 'Its teeth are very long,' he said. 'Was it male or female?'

'Male,' the man said.

'They all want to see it. Can I show it to them?'

'No. Put it back now.'

'They say it could be the last one in the forest,' the boy said, looking at the head dripping alcohol. He passed a finger over the yellow teeth, turned it this way and that, and finally put it back. He topped up the jar with alcohol.

The man glanced at him. 'Enough of that,' he said. 'Put the jar away.'

The boy did as he was told. He sat down and began to shell the maize moodily, while his eyes travelled around the small house. 'You shouldn't be doing this,' he said. 'Not you. You saved the village from the jaguar. None of them could have killed it. They ought to have picked our maize for us. To show they're grateful.'

The man went to the far end of the room where the kitchen was: a bench, some pots and glasses, a water tank with a tap over a plastic bowl to wash one's hands and a Styrofoam cool-box. He poured himself a glass of water and drank it, staring out of the door. His wife was chopping wood for the fire with the machete. The dog came wagging its tail, but it did not dare cross the threshold.

'Are you going to teach me how to shoot?' the boy asked. 'I have to learn, no? If I am to take your place when you — ' He was going to say 'die', but shied away from saying the word, the way his mother never spoke of the Devil. Ever since the jaguar had attacked him, death had stopped being too far away in the future, unthinkable. He said instead, 'If I am to take your place when the time comes.'

The Indian came away from the door. The big heap of maize ears still waiting to be shelled was taking most of the room: the family would have to sleep outside that night. The boy was working slowly, without concentration, looking up at his father now and then. The man thought: he is a good boy. I have to be a good father to him. He said, 'Go and get the gun. There won't be light for much longer.'

They went behind the house, with the boy carrying the rifle. The man set up an empty tin for a target, and said, 'I don't have many cartridges. You can have three shots. When I go to the town to sell the skin I'll buy more, and you'll get to shoot again.' The boy struggled with the bolt, which was too stiff for him. The man took the gun and bolted it himself. He said, 'Don't worry about that. When you are a little older you'll be strong enough to do it easily.' He remembered the squatters struggling to climb up the steep muddy slope while he bolted the rifle, aimed, fired and bolted the rifle again . . .

The boy said, 'Can I shoot now?' The man

looked at him. The boy — yes, the boy. He would do anything so that one day the boy would be a better leader of their people than he had been. He gave him the rifle back, then stood behind him and, supporting most of the weight of the rifle himself, showed the boy how to rest it against his shoulder and take aim. The woman had stopped chopping wood and watched them. The Indian glanced at her: there was no pride in her stare. A heavy sense of shame came over him, and he thought: she knows, she knows . . . He shut his eyes. His hands felt sticky and wet against the wooden stock. There was the crack of the rifle, and a sudden backward movement pushed the boy hard against his chest. The man held the little body in his arms for a long while, tightly, as if he were shielding it from all the evils of the world.

14

The man and the boy slept on mats on the ground under the stars. It was still night, but Hortensia got up and wrapped herself in her shawl. That was how her day always began ever since she was a child: one moment she was asleep and the next on her feet, busying herself with her chores. The only change in her routine these days had been the brief prayer that she whispered, kneeling down with eyes shut before dressing. When she finished praying and had dressed, she took the machete and went to cut wood for the fire. It was never quiet in the forest — unless there was danger around. The monkeys' shadows moved about in the trees, making the leaves rustle as the first light of day began to appear.

She had gone some way before turning around and coming back to the house in a hurry. She shook Venustiano by the shoulder and whispered, pointing towards the forest, 'They're coming. Quick. They aren't far.' The Indian jumped up and picked up his rifle. She gave him the machete. 'Go and hide them,' she said. The Indian went and hid the gun and the machete under the drying maize. 'Are you going to tell the others?' she said. His head was turned towards the direction in the forest from which the woman had come.

'Wake the boy up,' he said.

She shook the boy and whispered to him. The boy sat up, rubbing his eyes, and looked at the man. The Indian said in a harsh voice, 'Go and get the priest.'

While the boy was gone, they heard the hooves squelching through the mud, and a group of men on muleback came out of the trees. They were riding tiredly, in no formation, dressed in olive-green uniforms without insignia, with their rifles slung across the chest. The man with the old Sten gun hanging down from the saddle stood out from them. His campesino hat did not go with his fatigues: it was a leader's privilege to be noticeable. The woman came and stood next to her husband, and they watched the approaching riders. The man with the Sten and the straw hat said, grinning, 'Wake up, wake up now.' He stopped in front of the couple and said with menacing bonhomie, 'Do you always sleep so late, you people?' He climbed down from the mule and his men did the same.

The sun, still out of sight of the village, turned the edges of the thick low clouds yellow. Back down the hill the villagers were coming out of their houses — the boy must have warned them. They stood there, looking from afar: they did not want to come near the guerrillas. Venustiano stared at the small lean figures among the thatched-roofed houses in the distance. He did not expect them to come to his rescue if anything bad happened — they were farmers, not warriors. He felt no contempt for them, just disappointment. Only the dogs showed some appetite for confrontation with their futile barking.

The man with the sub-machine gun said, 'Let's go down to the village and meet the rest. You Indians are a shy bunch, aren't you?' The Indian couple walked ahead of the armed men and their mules. There was very little clanking or snorting; it was as if the animals had learned to imitate the furtiveness of their riders. The group came down the hill and into the middle of the village. The dogs fled to the far end of the street and were still barking, but no one paid any attention. Father Thomas appeared at the door of the church followed by the boy, and came quickly towards the gathered men, putting on his shirt on the way. The tongues of his boots hung down heavily, he had not done up the laces or put on his socks. He came up to the man with the Sten and said, 'Why are you here?'

'Is there going to be a Mass today, Father?' the man said.

'No.'

'One wonders how you spend your days.' He looked left and right, but neither the Indians nor any of his men laughed. The smile went from his face and he stood touching the Sten gun, embarrassed: he was like a comedian performing to an audience who did not share his sense of humour.

Venustiano said, 'What do you want?'

The guerrilla turned to the gathering and said, raising his voice, 'There are four men missing. Farmers. It's been more than a month.' The Indians stared at him as if they had not understood. They kept close to their houses, whose flimsy wooden walls could not possibly offer them any protection against gunfire. Milagros was among them. The guerrilla's eyes fell on her with curiosity and then abruptly moved away: he did not want to give the wrong impression; a leader ought to set an example to his men. He said, 'Has any one of you seen them? They were working in the forest not far from here. I know you don't like the farmers — or us, for that matter. But they are poor men like you, with families.' There was silence. He looked at the crowd, who looked back with inscrutable faces. A very light rain began to fall in the sunshine. There was no village square, just the single-room huts on either side of the mud track that ran from one end of the settlement to the other. The guerrilla ordered his men to search the houses. The priest said, 'What do you expect to find?'

'It will only take a minute, Father.'

No one else complained. While his men were searching, their leader asked, 'Who's the head of this village?'

'I am,' Venustiano said.

'Do you have anything to say?'

'We haven't seen them. We mind our business.'

'What business is that?'

'Farming the land back there.' The Indian motioned with his head towards the maize fields.

'The poor farmers,' the guerrilla said, 'farm the land too.' He looked at the crowd again and said, 'You should be helping each other. Stop trying to have the farmers thrown out of the forest.' The Indians said nothing, and he went on. 'The forest doesn't belong to you or me. Everyone who can make a living out of it should be allowed to come here. The government says that farming is destroying the forest. We'll make sure that doesn't happen. Don't you farm the land too? Have you destroyed the forest? You say you've been here for hundreds of years . . . Oh, the day the government gives some of the land beyond the forest back to the poor farmer, no one will ever come here again.' He looked around and said to the priest, 'It isn't quite paradise, is it now?' He spoke with great conviction: if he could only make the Indians understand. He kept his eyes on the priest and said, 'Greed is a great sin. Isn't it, Father? Go on, tell these people about it.' A couple of guerrillas standing behind him seemed bored: one fiddled about with his gun, another kept picking his nose; they must have heard it all before, and it was tedious, as much as it was true. Their leader said, 'You haven't done a good job, Father. What's the point of having a church here if you can't teach those people how to be good Christians?' He scanned the silent crowd. 'If anything happened to those farmers,' he said, 'if you did anything bad, I swear . . . '

Father Thomas said, 'Do these huts seem like the homes of greedy people to you?'

The men who had gone to search the houses came back. One was carrying Venustiano's rifle. The man with the Sten turned away from the priest and took the old gun in his hands. He opened the bolt, made sure that it was unloaded and held it up. He said, 'Whose is this? Anyone else have one? I didn't know you had firearms. Speak up.'

Venustiano was only a few feet away. He said, 'It's mine.'

'Where did you get it?'

'It was my grandfather's.'

'Have you shot anyone with it?'

'No.'

'What do you do with it?'

'I go hunting.'

'Ah. When did you go last?'

'A week ago.'

'Did you come across any farmers, by any chance?'

'No.'

A guerrilla said almost humorously, as if he did not think it was important, 'There's a covered hole behind the animal pen, comandante. It looks like a grave, but there's no cross. It isn't very old.'

The guerrilla leader frowned. He asked the Indian, 'Who's buried there? Is this where you bury your people? By the pen?'

'No,' the Indian said.

'Who then? Are you going to tell me?'

'A cow.'

'A cow, eh?'

'Yes.'

The guerrilla gave him a lingering look. 'Don't you eat the animals you kill?' he said. He turned to his men while still addressing the Indian. 'Did you give it a funeral, too?' This time his men laughed, and he went on, 'Did the father put you up to it? It wouldn't surprise me.'

'The jaguar killed it. We let it rot.'

'Ah, I see,' the guerrilla said. 'The jaguar. Yes, someone told me about that. Well, let's dig it up.' The whole gathering went to the edge of the village, where a few Indians set about digging at the place behind the pen. The other villagers looked on with intense curiosity as if they did not know what the diggers were going to unearth. Finally when the rotting carcase covered with maggots came to light, everyone stepped back and pinched their noses. A look of disgust crossed the guerrilla leader's face, and he gave the order to cover the animal back up. He stood with his thumb hooked in the Sten's sling: he had hoped that the Indian would have lied to him. A vulture circled above; it had smelt the rotten flesh. The man with the Sten walked back towards the centre of the village. Everyone followed him, as if willingly (he had not ordered them to do so), staring at him, trying to guess what he was thinking. As they approached the church he saw the crude cross stuck in the ground behind the building. Immediately he said, 'And who's buried over there?' He went towards it. 'Well, it's too small for a cow.' He stood on the edge of the grave and said in a mocking voice, 'Who is it this time? A man? A woman? Or a dog?'

The priest was only a few steps away. For a moment he thought that the danger had passed, but now his fear came back. He mulled over what he might say. He was filled with an overwhelming sense of responsibility — he struggled not to let it turn into guilt, for it had been his decision to bury the lieutenant in the village. Would the comandante believe him, if he told him that the dead was some white man other than a soldier? As he took a step forward, he heard Onésimo say, 'It was a man from here. The jaguar killed him in the forest.'

The guerrilla stopped smiling. He said, 'I'm sorry to hear it. It's not that I don't believe you, but I'd still like to have a look.'

The Indians stood by, saying nothing. It was as if they were not worried at all, just resigned to what was going to happen. Even Venustiano turned silent after that. The priest glanced in his direction: he avoided meeting the man's eye. The priest said, 'Comandante, please.'

'What is it, Father?'

The priest came closer and whispered to his ear, 'The dead man's wife is watching. It'd be horrible . . . you understand.'

A dog made its way through the crowd, sniffing at the feet of Indians and guerrillas alike. The villagers with the spades stood by, waiting. The clouds travelled across the horizon, and the distant mountains slowly faded into the lead colour of the sky. A little blush of charity tinted the comandante's face. He said, 'I suppose it isn't necessary. It was meant to be — standard procedure. If you were in our place, Father, you'd understand. It's hard to trust anyone. We only want to help those whom no one else is helping.' He turned to the Indians with the spades. 'You aren't needed any more. Go home.' He turned towards the rest of the gathering. 'All of you.' He stared broodily into the distance, then said, looking at no one in particular, 'We need to search the area. With your permission we'll stay here for a couple of days.'

★   ★   ★

There were light footsteps outside and a small shadow was framed by the door. A young voice said, 'Father, are you awake?'

The priest lay awake in bed in the oppressive heat. He sat up and searched in the dark for his boots: you could not trust not to step on a scorpion. He said, 'Come in' while putting them on. The shadow trembled in the weak yellow light of the citronella candle burning on the table.

'Did I wake you up, Father?' the boy said.

'No. It's too hot to sleep.'

The boy took a step into the room and stopped: his tunic stood like a white stain in the dark. He said matter-of-factly, 'I have a question.' The smell of his sweat spread across the room: it was not a grown-up's unpleasant smell; it was as if innocence had its own scent. Outside a large round moon was obscured by motionless clouds, and the air was heavy with hot vapour. It must have been not long after midnight. You could tell the time in the forest by the degree of humidity: it peaked just before dawn. The priest made room for the boy to sit on the bed, but the white tunic did not move from where it was. Out behind the church the cross over the lieutenant's grave was barely visible.

'Couldn't wait until the morning?' the priest said, and immediately regretted the way it had sounded — he had not meant to be brusque. He added, 'I don't mind. It's nice to have company. Are you worried about something?'

'Yes.'

'The guerrillas?'

The boy hesitated, then said unexpectedly,

'If I die now, will I go to hell, Father?'

'Why do you say that?'

'Tell me.'

'No, you won't. You'll go to paradise.'

'Even though I haven't had Communion yet?'

'Oh, that. Well, you've been baptised, haven't you? A child who hasn't reached the age of reason can't sin. He's in what is called a state of grace.' The words came to him without thinking. He had said them so many times before: perhaps he was not any less cynical than the bishop after all.

The boy watched him intently, as if he spoke in a language that the boy had trouble understanding. The boy nodded, even though the answer did not seem to have calmed him down much. 'Thank you, Father,' he said. 'My mother will be happy.'

'Did she send you?'

'She didn't know the answer. She told me to ask you.'

'In the middle of the night?'

'I have to go now.' He did not move. He lingered at the door, waiting for something: he was like a guest hoping for an invitation to stay longer.

The priest said, 'Perhaps you'll sleep better now that you know.'

'No, no, I'm not going to bed, Father,' the

boy said as if he had heard something absurd. The priest poured himself a glass of water. He said, 'Where are you going at this hour?'

There was a little persistent noise outside — some animal rummaging through the grass along the wall of the house.

'In the forest,' the boy said. 'With Father.'

'In the forest? Why?'

'I know my mother told you about the settlers. We have to bury them before the guerrillas find them.'

'Can't he get some man to go with him?'

'They won't go. They told him it was he who killed the squatters and he should do it himself.'

The priest said, 'You're still limping.'

'Oh, it's nothing. We aren't going too far.'

As he sat listening to the child, Father Thomas thought of the time when, as a young priest right after seminary, he taught for a few summers at a school for deaf-mute boys run by the Church. The school had been on the south coast of England, and going there was a good way to have a holiday and do something for the children too. He had taught himself sign language and the teaching was not demanding: basic calculus and geography a couple of hours a day, and the rest of the time he was free: he would go for a swim early in the morning and again as the sun went down. He remembered his rooms — a bedroom and a study — as being plain but delightful; the red-brick Victorian buildings, the smell of wax from the old uneven floorboards, the freshness of the sheets, the nuns going about with their hands hidden in the sleeves of their habits, the cool draught blowing in through the big windows facing the sea.

The students were obliged to come to confession once a week, one of the strict rules that he had not contested, with the excuse to himself that he was only a visitor who came for a couple of months a year and did not have the right to challenge the way the school was run. At least the boys liked him, because he was young back then and approachable, so it had seemed to him that they did not mind spending a few minutes with him in the confessional. A boy came to see him, one of the quiet ones — do they always choose the shy ones because they are less likely to talk? There was no latticework in the confessional, of course: they could only communicate through signs. The boy gestured without looking at him, something about lying in bed in the night and the director touching him. He understood at once. He asked: when did it happen? More than once? He had not heard of similar stories before, but despite his naivety he did not doubt the boy at all. One would not make up a story like that. Did the nuns know? No, the boy did not think so. Had it happened to other boys too? The boy nodded and gave him some names . . . He watched, and his anger grew in the narrow wooden confessional.

The director of the school was Father Sebastian, a charming man who had made him feel at home when he had first come to the school. He took his holidays, usually somewhere abroad, soon after the young teacher came, but he was always there to greet him before going off. The firm handshake, the pat on the back, the taut ruddy cheeks and boyish close-cropped hair on the ageing face: Father Thomas could not help but like the director. Only his coiffed forelock, he seemed to remember, had struck him as rather vain at the time, but his admiration for him forgave that minor sin. He went to see the director about the student's revelations, expecting an angry confrontation, but Father Sebastian smiled and shook his head in mock despair. Stories, what stories these boys make up . . . And he sat back in his chair and smiled and smiled like a benevolent father. Then he asked the young priest for the name of the boy who had made those silly claims, but Father Thomas refused to tell him. The man had not liked it. He had launched into a long explanation of why boys in institutions like his came up with things like that — it was out of dullness, you see, a way to create some excitement, have something to talk about. He, Father Thomas, had not much experience of a place like that. If he had been there for as long as he had . . . On and on he went, and Father Thomas listened. Sometime later, while the man was still speaking, he had got up and walked out.

He now looked at the Indian boy standing half in shadow. He had such great respect for the priesthood back then, he could not have imagined that a priest would hurt a child like that. He had reported the director, but nothing had come of it, and when he had enquired about it, he had been told not to take the matter any further. They had suggested that it would cause the Church great damage. He had done as he had been told — when he had become a priest he had taken a vow of obedience. He would have been risking his place in the Church otherwise. How devoted to them he had been — a young idealist. Since then he had tried to convince himself that, now that his behaviour was no longer a secret, Father Sebastian would stop, but he had never found out what had happened. He had resigned his teaching post and had never gone back to the school. He was a coward.

A few insects braved the smell of citronella and buzzed around the room. The animal outside the window kept making its little noise, methodical and discreet like a beggar going through a rubbish bin.

'Aren't you afraid?' the priest said.

'No,' the boy said hesitantly. 'You said if I die I'll go to heaven. Isn't it true, Father?'

'Yes, yes.'

'Then there's no reason to be afraid, no? It's only that it's so many of them. If it were two or three . . . My father would kill them very easily, I know he would. He's very brave. He killed the jaguar, didn't he?'

He shook with fear. The priest said, 'You shouldn't go. Perhaps the guerrillas won't come across the bodies. It's so difficult to find something in the forest, even if you know where to look for it.'

The boy dismissed his suggestion, shaking his head. He said, 'It needs to be done, Father. I have to go.' He added, as if repeating something that he had been told to memorise, 'It is my duty. One day I'll be the head of this village.'

'Let me speak to your father. Perhaps there is a way. The guerrillas might see you go.'

'They won't. They've camped at the other

end of the village.'

'Good, good,' the priest said. He was thinking. 'Let's go and see your father.'

'Why?'

The priest got up and coaxed the boy out of the room. 'There isn't much time. It'll be daylight soon.'

'Are you going to come with us, Father?'

'With you?'

'To the forest. To bury the dead.'

'I'll go with your father. You stay at home.'

'Ah.' The boy did not speak for a while, then he said, 'Yes, I understand. It's different for you, Father. If you die you'll become a saint.'

15

The shade of the trees blocked the sun from drying the mud through which the two men plodded. It had rained heavily for a while after they had set off, and the mud was slowing them down. They were on foot, the priest pulling his mule along the narrow path, which became more difficult to follow the farther they went. The path disappeared in the soft mud, the pools of rainwater and the bushes, which grew over it; only someone very familiar with it could pick it up farther along. Suddenly it began to rain again. There had been no thunder, no scattered drops that come before a shower or cool wind, just sudden rain, which fell over the forest, silencing the birds and monkeys. Neither of the two men was dressed for it, but they did not look for shelter, they went on. The rain stopped as suddenly as it had started, and now the forest smelt of wet wood.

The priest sloshed through the mud several steps behind the Indian, who was clearing a path. He did not seem to struggle much. The priest swung his own machete at a few branches that the Indian's blade had missed and walked on. It was dawn, but the sky was still dark: the clouds were heavy. The priest helped the mule climb over a rock as the small figure in the white tunic disappeared into the darkness of the forest up ahead. Father Thomas called out, 'Wait for me,' and the Indian briefly stood still, then went out of sight and the chop-chop of his machete began again. The priest followed the path among the hacked-down bushes and vines.

Farther on the vegetation grew sparse and there was no path; the Indian could have gone in any direction without having to use his machete to clear his way. The priest called out his name several times, but the only answer he got was from a monkey, howling at him. The priest began to worry: perhaps the Indian had had a change of heart — or something might have happened to him. He picked a direction to follow and went on. He sheathed his machete, then drew it out again. It felt like some crude talisman: it would not protect him against the bullets, but it gave him a moderate sense of security. The ground was carpeted with leaves, which stuck to his boots, and he walked on noisily. A sense of betrayal stirred in him, as though everything he had done for the Indians had not mattered at all. But what exactly had he done? Perhaps this was a fitting way to end his time in the forest — to know that he was not needed, that he would not be missed. He had been walking for some time when he returned his machete to its sheath and began to think that he ought to turn back.

He decided to go a little farther still. At the foot of a hill he heard the distant noise of water and pulled the mule towards it. The Indian was waiting on the other side of the stream. When he saw the priest, he raised his hand, but said nothing: it was as if they had made an appointment there. Father Thomas crossed the stream and said to the Indian, 'I lost you back there.'

'Well,' the other man said, 'I was waiting here.'

'Is this the place?'

The Indian pointed at a hillside nearby. The priest tethered the mule and went to have a look. The dead lay where they had fallen, their clothes soaked in rain and their faces covered in mud. The heavy smell of the damp forest stifled the stench of rotten flesh. He did not look at the faces, but recognised, from his cap, the old squatter he had met. This was not a funeral with the dead dressed in a formal suit. The flowers, the marble slab, the carved inscription painted in gold: in death everyone had the right to be treated like a hero, but this was just ugliness, meaninglessness.

They had to get to work without delay if they were to be back in the village before the guerrillas suspected them. They found a place among the trees large enough to accommodate the four bodies, took the spades from the mule and began. The earth was easy to dig — it was covered only in grass and was soft underneath because of the rain. They covered the pit and the priest said a brief prayer. He had not brought the Mass kit with the holy water along, but it did not really matter. He was doing all that for the Indian's benefit or, rather, for the sake of the priest who would come to the forest after him; to the Indians, a Christian priest was a shaman in contact with the spirit world. He filled his canteen from the stream and sprinkled the earth with water, making the sign of the Cross. Then he heard the sound of an animal moving nearby. He paused with the canteen in his hands and looked at the Indian: he had unslung his rifle and stood staring into the forest, saying nothing; suddenly he was a hunter. He waved the priest to be quiet and walked softly into the forest — he wanted to hunt alone.

★ ★ ★

It was not very far away. Venustiano had guessed what it was from the noise. After a while he picked up the strong odour of the animal marking its territory — he was close. There was the crushing sound again: the animal was eating. A sense of excitement came over the Indian. He had not hunted anything for food in a while. The jaguar had been different — more like an act of revenge.

He was glad to be away from the priest and the place they had buried the squatters. It had been hard to look at the rotting flesh, the empty eyes, the mouths frozen open — even the priest's silence had felt like an accusation. The ground was strewn with leaves and twigs, and he had to move very slowly to avoid them crackling under his feet — a few steps, then a pause to hear whether the animal had heard him, then a few more steps forward again. When he felt the urge to cough, he held his breath to smother it, and he was afraid that the animal had heard, but it continued to shuffle about, eating.

He had been angry at his son for telling the priest about their mission, but now he was glad that the boy had stayed behind — safe. What he did not like was the foreigner blaming him for the situation they were now in. He could tell, even though the father had not said a word about it. But he knew that he had done the right thing — considering. There were times when any decision one took was wrong. He would sacrifice himself if it would help his people.

The pungent smell left by the animal on the bushes was stronger now. He bolted the rifle and went on, starting and stopping every few steps. But his mind was not on the hunt: he was thinking about the dead men again. Something moved nearby, and the Indian started. It was nothing, just a bird in a tree, but he remembered his grandfather telling him how, after burial, a dead man's soul goes to the underworld while his body becomes a ghost, which haunts the places where the dead man used to live. Oh, his grandfather was a wise man. How he wished that he were alive to tell him what to do now . . . He took a few more steps and a chattering noise came from the direction of the trees: the animal had heard him.

The peccary was in a little clearing some forty yards away, looking in his direction. He stood still; the small animal could not see well at a distance. He waited until it went back to digging the ground, and then he rested the rifle against his shoulder and aimed. Then the ghosts were again in his mind — the squatters running away from him as he took aim at each of them in turn. He fired, keeping his eyes shut, and when he looked again he saw the peccary running into the trees. He reloaded and quickly fired again, this time with one eye open. The bullet struck a tree near its target, and the animal disappeared into the woods. He did not shoot again. He turned and went back to where he had left the priest, walking with slow heavy strides.

★   ★   ★

Father Thomas watched the Indian emerge from the trees with the rifle slung over his shoulder. He was surprised to see that he was not carrying an animal: everyone said that he was a great hunter — he had proved it by killing the jaguar. The priest fetched the mule, and they started on the path back to the village. The clouds had cleared and the sun was heating up the forest, turning the rainwater on the trees and the ground into steam, which rose up in the air. The Indian walked ahead with a sullen face. The priest had hoped that the burial would have been the Indian's chance to feel remorse. He saw no sign of that, but one never knew what that man was thinking. He thought of the decomposing bodies lying in the mud, and the Indian staring at them with what had seemed to him like impatience. Had he taken pleasure in killing them? Watching him watching the dead had felt to the priest like flashing a torch at some people involved in an ugly act: vandalising a house or tormenting an animal or making love in a filthy place — ugliness was best enjoyed in privacy and with a burden of guilt. He had derived no satisfaction from having come to help the Indian bury the dead; in fact he had hated it. Now that their task was over he wanted to get back as soon as possible, back to the small room in the back of the church and his bed. He paid no attention to the landscape. The forest used to hold a great attraction for him once, but the recent violence had made it ugly and hostile. Still he would have liked to stay — if only so that he would not have to go back home.

Suddenly a shot struck a tree near them. For a moment both men stood there, not knowing what to do: they were unsure where the shot had come from, ahead or behind them — then there was another crack of a rifle and a second bullet coming from ahead of them whistled past. They turned and ran away from it, back in the direction they had come from, with the priest pulling the mule. It had been foolish to go after that animal, he thought; the Indian's shots had betrayed their presence. He wondered whether somehow the other man had wanted to challenge his fate.

They ran deeper into the forest, farther away from the village, expecting more shots to be fired at them. None came, but they plunged into the ferns, assuming they were still being pursued. Suddenly the mule locked its feet and refused to move. The priest tugged at its reins furiously, but no matter what he did it would not move. The Indian stared on with his blank expression, saying nothing. The priest cut a shoot from a tree and whipped the mule, which jerked from the pain and its foot landed on his. He dropped the switch and let out a cry as his foot was driven into the mud. When he tried to move, it hurt him badly. He waved the Indian away. He said, 'Don't wait for me.' The other man looked in the direction they had come from, but did not move.

'What are you waiting for?' the priest said. 'Better hurry. I'll follow.'

'We should go together.'

'I can't run. I'll hide somewhere.'

'Come,' the other man said. 'Get on the mule.'

'The mule won't move,' the priest said. 'Leave it alone.'

'I know a place. Can you walk at all?'

'I don't know. Oh, it hurts. If it isn't . . . '

He did not really want to stay behind. He took a step: the pain was bearable. He said, 'I won't be able to go far.'

'It isn't far,' the Indian said. They heard something now — some distance away the monkeys howling: the guerrillas could be coming. The Indian said in a harsh voice, 'I won't let them find you.'

Father Thomas shook his head. 'Don't worry about me. We'll go in different directions. I'll find somewhere to hide. What sort of a place is it you want us to go to? I won't be able to get there . . . But I thank you.' Their pursuers must have come across the fresh grave. If he had not been a coward he would have stayed behind to try and reason with them.

'There isn't time . . . ' the Indian said.

'Fine, fine. Let's go.'

Not very far from where they had abandoned the mule, they came across large mossy stones peeking out of the undergrowth and toppled walls held down by tree roots. As they entered a paved stepped plaza it began to rain again. The Indian led the way, searching around the half-buried ancient buildings for somewhere to hide. Hidden behind some bushes there was a small opening among the blocks of stone. The priest had a torch and he flashed it into the dark as they climbed down some steps to a damp room. He moved the beam carefully about: he could only see stone walls and pools of water on the floor. They sat down near the entrance. 'Who knows of this place?' he said.

'No one.'

'Not even your people?'

'I discovered it some time ago, but told no one.'

'Milagros would be very interested to know . . . '

'Don't tell her.'

The rain poured outside as they sat on the floor in silence. 'Could those out there be squatters?' the priest asked.

The Indian shook his head. 'Guerrillas.'

'Maybe they recognised us. We have to go back to the village to warn the people.'

The Indian said sensibly, 'Don't talk. Maybe they are nearby.' He looked nervously in the direction of the entrance. The priest wondered whether the other man had heard anything — all he could hear himself was the sound of the rain. Drops plopped onto the ground from the roof. The two men stared at the slice of daylight coming through the narrow entrance.

After a long time of having heard nothing the priest said, 'Do you think they're still about?'

'We'll wait a little longer,' the Indian said.

'Then I'll go and see.' He held the rifle sombrely in his arms.

The priest was convinced that the people out there were gone, but then he heard them. It seemed they were going through the buildings one by one. He went to look for another way out, splashing across the pools of rainwater. Some distance away the room abruptly ended in a pile of rubble. He flashed the torch all around, but there was no opening among the faded murals on the walls. He was not in a hurry to return with the bad news. He looked at the ancient images. They were scenes of execution and public torture: fingernails being pulled, fingers cut off, limbs broken, jaws torn off from captives still alive . . . A celebration of violence or some religious ceremony perhaps.

The Indian whispered from the other end of the darkness, 'Is there a way out?'

'No.' The priest came back to the entrance and sat down next to the Indian. Water dripped on him and he moved a little closer to the other man so that their shoulders touched, as the drops turned into a steady trickle. 'It's very cold to stay long in here,' the priest said. 'Maybe we should make a run for it.'

'No. It isn't safe.'

They sat with their shoulders touching.

231

There was a muffled blast: the priest started and put the torch out. Somewhere out there their pursuers had perhaps discovered the entrance to some building and had thrown a grenade before going in. He did not move or put the torch on again. They stayed in the dark, listening to the water trickling down from the roof. There was another dull explosion somewhere and, seized with fear, he stood up and put on the torch again. Its beam travelled across the collapsed blocks of stone at the end of the hall, bringing back no hope.

'Sit down, Father,' the Indian said as though to a child, and the priest put the torch out and obeyed. Their shoulders no longer touched: the moment of intimacy had passed. Voices came from outside — closer than the earlier blasts, but still not very near. The searchers were thorough, going from place to place, making their way towards them without hurry. The unpleasant smell of dampness settled over the two men like a veil. The Indian said, 'Aren't you going to pray?' Father Thomas could not tell whether it was said mockingly. Through the door a little sunlight shone: a sign that the storm had moved on; the guerrillas' search would now be easier. 'You don't really believe in Hesuklisto, Father, do you?' the Indian said.

'Why do you say that?'

'If you did, you'd ask him to help us — my people, I mean.'

'How about you? Don't you want him to help you too?'

'No god cares for those who won't bow to him. But the woman and the boy go to the house of your god, and he ought to help them.'

The priest listened to the Indian talk about his wife and son with love. To love a person like that was something he had never experienced. He had dismissed it so easily when he was young. He used to believe that true kindness was silent, uncommitted; unlike erotic love, which needed words and waited for something in return, like an explorer in the Age of Discovery handing out tawdry gifts to tribesmen. So he had chosen to love God instead, and had done it with passion, but God had given little in return, like a capricious lover, demanding this and that, never satisfied. He sat with his back to the damp wall and said, 'We should go back as soon as we get the chance. We have to warn the people.'

'We have to wait,' the Indian said.

His foot was hurting more now, even when he put no weight on it. He took off his boot and saw that his ankle was badly swollen:

perhaps it was broken. The village felt as if it were too far away ... Suddenly there was laughing and shouting outside. The Indian went to the door and looked out. The priest hobbled over to him, but saw nothing, either. The voices seemed to be coming from close by. Then something began to squeal. The two men took a few cautious steps out of their hiding place and peeked through the shrubs: the plaza was filled with guerrillas who had put their weapons aside and were chasing a peccary. The little animal was going round and round like a clockwork toy; they had blocked its way out and it could not run into the forest. The two men returned to their hiding place.

'I suppose this means they don't know we are here,' the priest said. 'They are searching the ruins just in case. We should make a run for it now.'

'Can you walk?'

'Yes, yes,' the priest said and tried to stand. A sharp pain made him wince, but he carefully moved towards the exit. The pain grew worse with each step. After a few feet he could stand it no more, and he sat down again. The Indian gave the priest his rifle. 'I will carry you. Lean on this.'

'No, it's foolish,' the priest said, but stood again with the help of the rifle. He tried to

234

lean on the Indian, but the young man was much smaller than him and could not really support him. The sun came through the narrow entrance, lighting up the mossy stones with a hard light while the shouting and the squealing continued outside.

'No, no, this won't do . . . ' the priest said. He stood propped uncomfortably on the rifle under the Indian's stare: there was no scorn in it, just impatience. Suddenly Venustiano knelt down, crossed himself and rested his folded hands on his forehead, the way he had seen the woman do. The priest looked at him in disbelief.

The Indian said, 'Pray to Hesuklisto to help us, Father.' The whole situation made perfect sense to him: the foreign god had great power over the forest after all, and was angry at him for the killings of the squatters because they had been Christians. But the father was a good man, and Hesuklisto could spare their lives if he so wished. The father had always said that his god could perform miracles — was not that what the peccary was? The Indian said in an uncertain voice, 'If you get your god to help my people, I will start coming to his house too.'

'I wish I could promise you that he would help you,' the priest said. He tried to stand again, but the pain in his foot took away all his strength and he fell down heavily.

The Indian glanced out of the door and asked, 'What do you want in return?'

'Nothing. God will do as He pleases. The best way to help your people now is to warn them. Then you ought to stay away from the village for a while.' He looked at his swollen foot with dismay.

The Indian said, 'What if I were to be baptised? I know your god likes that. I could order everyone to be baptised.'

'Well, there's no need to force anyone. Perhaps one day you'll decide to do it of your own volition.'

The Indian clenched his fists and said, 'You won't ask him to help us because you want to punish me.'

The priest watched him with understanding. How could he convince him that there was no god out there who punished people, no force of good or evil, no one to hear their prayer, nothing, nothing . . . He could not tell him that God was just an idea: love — a way of living that was impossible in this world. 'We don't have time,' he said. 'Go now. Get everyone out of the village.'

'And you?'

'I'll follow when I get the chance.'

The narrow Indian eyes stared suspiciously at him. 'If you have some plan . . . '

'What sort of plan?'

'Are you going to speak to them? After I'm gone? Try to do a deal?'

'I'm not going to speak to anyone. I'll wait until they're gone and make my way to the village somehow. Don't wait for me. Get the people as far away as you can.'

'Where can we go? The guerrillas will find us.'

'Well, you could go to the town.'

'The town? No. What are we going to do there?'

'It's the only place you'd be safe from them.'

'I'd rather fight them.'

The sound of shouting and laughter travelled in from the direction of the plaza, mocking the Indian's desperate bravado. He said stubbornly, 'You shouldn't stay behind. We'll go together.'

'We'll be wasting time, and risking our lives and those of your people, too.'

'No. Come.'

He took hold of the priest under the armpits and helped him to his feet. This time Father Thomas was careful not to put any weight on his injured foot. He was surprised that he could walk slowly and without too much pain — if only he had a better crutch than the rifle. They took a couple of steps together, then suddenly he felt that he did not want to leave. It was selfish of him to be risking the lives of everyone in the village. If he were not a coward, really not a coward, he would let the Indian go quickly back and warn the people. He began to repeat silently to himself, 'I am not a coward, I am not a coward . . . ' and, pretending to lose his balance, he slipped off the Indian's hands and dropped to the ground. The sharp pain pleased him — it was as if someone had dared him to do it. He dragged himself against the wall and waved the other man away.

The Indian said, 'Come, get up again.'

'No. It's impossible. I'm sorry.'

'Come, Father,' the Indian said with irritation, and bent down. 'You have to try again.'

'No use. It hurts too much. Don't you care about your people, man? You have to save them. There's no point wasting any more time. Go.' He put his hand on the Indian's shoulder and said, feeling weak and frightened, 'I'll be fine. I'll just stay here until they're gone. It's safe.'

The Indian looked at him for another moment and picked up his rifle. He went out of the buried building and towards the trees, away from the plaza where the joyful shouting continued. As he was reaching the trees, the peccary began to squeal wildly — a moment later there was silence. The priest hobbled to the door and looked out. In the plaza the shouting had died down and the men crowded round the small dark mass on the ground. Someone was holding a knife. On the edge of the forest the Indian paused to look back at the priest and quickly disappeared into the trees. In the plaza the man with the knife raised up the lifeless little animal for everyone to see, like a warrior in the past holding the scalp of a dead enemy.

16

It had been quiet for a while. The priest hopped to the door: there was no one out in the plaza. He came cautiously out of the building and looked around for a stick to use as a crutch. When he found one he went towards the plaza. There was a little bloodstain on the grassy flagstones where the peccary had been killed. It was like the remains of a ritualistic sacrifice, an offering to the gods to spare the lives of the Indian and himself. The pain in his foot was almost bearable now, but he did not dare let it touch the ground. He slowly made his way to the forest with the crutch under his arm, trying to remember which way he had come from earlier that day. There was no wind: the droplets of humidity hanging in the air stuck to his skin like flies. He quickly got used to the crude crutch and walked confidently with it, without looking down at the uneven ground, but nevertheless his progress was very slow; at this rate he would not be in the village until late at night. Howling broke out from the monkeys passing on the warning of his presence. As the sun touched the top of the mountains he thought about coming across the wounded lieutenant with the young, mistrustful face, weeks before. What would have happened if the squatters had come across him instead? How impossible the concept of loving one's enemy was — a trap of the conscience that so often went against common sense. All this would not have happened if he had just given the soldier his mule and sent him in the direction of the town. The lieutenant would almost certainly have died before he got there, of course — but had he not died after all? And now the Indians would have to abandon their village.

Up ahead the forest opened up and the path began to slope down. At the bottom of the hill he continued across a flat area of land covered with thorny bushes coming up to his waist. The place did not seem familiar: he was probably lost; the thought filled him with dread. If he did not find his way to the village soon, he would not have the strength to get there at all — or he might end up coming across the guerrillas again. Suddenly there was a snort, and he saw his mule standing in the bushes a few yards away. He almost cried for joy. If he believed in miracles . . . He took hold of its reins and stroked its forehead, then leaned against it, threw away the crutch and climbed on with great effort. He had a better view of the forest from the mule's back, and could make a better guess at which direction to follow. It was still light, he ought to make the most of it; he kicked the mule and it broke into a trot. The forest felt empty despite the noises of the birds and the animals, but it was not reassuring; he knew it was a false impression. He kept looking behind him for any sign of the guerrillas. He thought: if I come across them . . . He tried to think of a plan in case he did: what to say, what tone of voice to use, how to convince them not to seek revenge. Perhaps his own ill feeling towards the squatters had been responsible for the deaths. If he had tried to mediate between the Indians and the squatters all those years, they might have found a way to live alongside each other. But he had always been a coward, did not get involved if there was any kind of risk. He had done it before, had kept silent. He took another look behind his back: nothing moved in the darkness of the path from which he had come.

He rode to the other end of the bush-covered land and went into the trees again. There was a smell of ash in the air. After a few minutes the trees abruptly ended, and a wide plateau that had been destroyed by fire spread out ahead of him. There was almost complete silence: nowhere for the birds and animals to hide, only beetles scurrying among the grass. He was reminded of his meeting with the squatters. This was the result of a fire like the one he had witnessed. No, he had not come this way before, now he was certain about it. Short grass already grew on the burnt ground: it was grazing land, but no cattle had fed here. He crossed what remained of a dirt track that had been washed away by the rains. The steep impassable slope was the reason why the pasture had been abandoned: it was cheap for a cattle farmer to hire a few squatters to burn down another piece of the forest close to another track. He left the burnt land behind and entered the virgin forest again, where the last light of the day did not penetrate. He used to enjoy travelling on his own, like in the time before coming across the lieutenant in the forest, but he was never truly happy being alone for long periods at a time, that was one of his weaknesses. Unexpectedly he began to think about happiness. In order to be blissfully happy one had to be ignorant of certain things. How could one be happy, day in and day out, when there was so much suffering in the world? It felt heartless to him. Even being in love meant one worried about another, one's happiness was marred by it.

He guided the mule over to a narrow parting in the dense vegetation that could have been a path once. He wished he could sing: it might drive out his fear. Somehow a memory of childhood came to his mind and with it the words of an old nursery rhyme: 'To market, to market to buy a fat pig . . . ' He sang it a few times before telling himself that he should be quiet. He went on in utter silence.

Suddenly he recognised the landscape: he was near the village. He did not hurry, but led the mule cautiously towards the distant houses. If he could have walked he would have got off the mule and continued on foot — the guerrillas might lie in ambush. There seemed to be no one about, but he found a spot in the trees that gave a good view of the houses, and he stayed there for some while, watching. The village seemed completely abandoned: the Indians were gone too. At last he came out of his hiding place and went towards the church. The sun had long come down behind the ridge of the mountains, but there was still a little light. He left the mule untethered in the street and went carefully in. He would not have been surprised if some guerrillas were inside after all and opened fire on him, but the church was empty. He packed a few clothes, his vestments and some food, and loaded them onto the mule — then he realised that he had not fed the animal since that morning, before leaving the village. He had had nothing to eat all day too and, after hanging the nosebag round the animal's neck, he took out some of the food that he had packed for himself.

The evening light faded: he should be going, the guerrillas could show up at any moment. The mule had to rest, but not there. Suddenly it brayed, and he hurried to calm it down, wondering what might have disturbed it. It could not have been the guerrillas: the mule was accustomed to human presence. Perhaps it was nothing, he thought, just the heat or the long walk. And, indeed, the animal turned quiet after a moment. The priest was anxious to go now: someone might have heard from afar.

He sat on the animal and urged it on, in the direction in which the Indians must have gone to escape the guerrillas. It was getting very dark — night fell fast in the forest. When he had first come to that place he had worn a watch, but then had realised that it served no purpose. The forest followed its own time: daybreak and dusk, the perfect darkness of the deep forest night, the hour when humidity peaked, the hour when the sweet smell of rotting leaves on the ground mixed with the fragrance of flowers. It all changed with the seasons, and one's routines had to adapt accordingly.

He felt safer when he reached the trees. He would ride for as long as he could see where he was going, he thought, and then would stop for the night. Once he turned the mule in the right direction, it picked its way through the mud and the rocks on the track without any guidance. He was eager to rejoin the Indians, to see Milagros, Hortensia and the boy again. He heard a sound, and immediately the mule stiffened and pricked up its ears. Man and animal stood silently in the near dark as his mind raced. Was it the guerrillas? There was no real need to ambush him. He was alone and unarmed; they could just shoot him or catch him easily. Perhaps it was some animal . . . The mule began to go backwards. He tried to get its mind off whatever it was that was frightening it by guiding it forwards, backwards, left and right. He could sense that the animal wanted to run. If he forced it to stay still, it would fight him and throw him off, so he let it move while trying to keep it under his control. While he was doing that he caught a glimpse of a yellow coat with dark spots disappearing into the dark undergrowth. Horror and disbelief came over him as he thought that it was impossible: the jaguar was dead. He pulled out his machete and compared in his mind the size of the animal he had just glimpsed with the skin of the one that the Indian had killed. This was much larger; and he had heard that young jaguars hunted with their mothers before going on their own. He raised his machete, ready to strike if she attacked.

He could not see her in the undergrowth; it was very dark, and he could not hear her, either. The mule snorted and stamped its feet, and he patted it on the shoulder, urging it forward, down the narrow path through the forest. It would not go: it could sense the danger had not gone. Suddenly a shadow darted out of the corner of his eye. When he turned, the jaguar was there, just a few feet away. The mule began to bray and kick and almost dropped him. As he struggled to stay on, the jaguar went for the mule's neck, but he swiped at her with the machete and she backed off. He pulled on the reins, but the mule did not obey. It continued to kick and went in this direction and that, looking for a way out of danger, turning back towards the direction from which they had come, and the priest had to hold onto the reins to keep his balance. Then, before he had fully steadied himself, the jaguar pounced on him.

He felt a violent pull just below his ribs,

and the pain made him drop the machete. For a split second he thought that she had bitten him and torn his jacket, then he realised that her teeth had taken a large piece of his flesh too. The jaguar backed off again: it was not after him. He reached instinctively for his wound. His fingers passed through the large tear in his jacket, but found nothing inside, then a little deeper inside he touched something soft and wet. The next time the mule lurched he had no strength to hold on, and he was flung off the saddle and onto the mud. Lying there, he saw the jaguar leap at the mule and bite it in the neck.

He looked round for the machete: it was several feet away. He made an attempt to move, but the pain was too much and he gave up. He dragged himself to a tree and sat with his back against it, taking care not to lean against his wound. The jaguar turned and looked at him calmly, her eyes indifferent and unafraid, catching the moonlight in the dark. She turned back to the dying mule and began to drag it towards the thickets. When she was out of his sight, the priest heard her eating; now that she had her prey she was not going to attack him again. He began to tremble. He felt cold, even though it was as hot and humid as any evening. He zipped up his jacket and hugged himself, but could not get warm. He wondered whether anyone would come for him. There was little chance of that: it would make no sense for the Indians to come back if they thought the guerrillas had caught up with him. In any case it would take some time before anyone would begin to worry about him. He wondered how long he would survive. He was losing a lot of blood: it was soaking through his clothes.

He thought about the Indians moving on, getting farther away from him with every minute, and he felt lonely — the loneliest he had felt in the forest. It was as if the whole world had forgotten him, and those who knew him were already going about their business with his memory never once crossing their mind. The feeling made him shudder, and he thought: if I make it back to the village, the guerrillas might help me when they come. He made another attempt to stand up, grabbing hold of the tree behind him with both hands. As soon as he tried, a sharp pain from his wound almost made him faint, and he dropped heavily back down. Was he going to die? He tried to shake the thought away. No, no, it wouldn't happen; he wasn't that bad, there was still hope. But the thought stayed with him . . . How many times he had gone to see someone who was dying — bedridden, their strength almost spent, a little light flickering in their eyes the only sign of life. Was it his turn this time? It would have done him good to have something to do while he waited for someone to come. The confession software that had so impressed him came to his mind again. It was something you put on your mobile phone, he remembered, to guide you through the admission of your sins and suggest suitable prayers. He chuckled — but he stopped because it made his chest hurt.

The jaguar was quiet: she must have finished eating. He was very weak, but the pain, which had been excruciating at first, had begun to subside, and a numbness was spreading across the whole of his body. He could not move his feet at all, no matter how much he tried. He tasted something metallic: blood trickled out of his mouth. The usual evening sounds of the forest had grown faint. It was as if he were in a church where everyone kept their voice down out of respect. Suddenly it turned altogether quiet. Something brushed against the grass, and the jaguar came out onto the path some distance away. He thought: If I'd let her have the mule, this wouldn't have happened. He did not know why he had done it — an act of bravado so that the Indians would admire him, or his pride telling him not to run away.

The jaguar came slowly towards him, walking softly on the mud, keeping her eyes fixed on him. She stopped some feet away and raised her head to sniff the air, then made a deep angry sound and showed her teeth at the priest. He felt the urge to look away, like a child who thinks that if he shuts his eyes the danger will disappear. He groped on the ground, but found nothing with which to defend himself. The jaguar came closer and stopped again, a short jump away from where he lay with his back against the tree. He could hear her rough breathing. Suddenly he began to cough: his throat was filled with blood, and he could not swallow. The jaguar snarled and then went unhurriedly into the undergrowth, as if she did not want to watch him die.

He waited for her to come back, but time passed and she did not return. It was late night now and he could see very little, only shadows. His mind concentrated on the sounds of the animals — anything to get his mind off the suffering. Something scratched nearby: another peccary perhaps. It knew he was there and did not come near. He felt exhausted. He had lost all feeling in his legs and was still spitting blood, but much less now. He thought: a life coming to an end like this, interrupted. He could have lived at least twenty, thirty years more. Twenty years: it felt like an eternity now — even that night seemed endless. The things he could have done if he had lived on. All this, lying there, bleeding to death, was of his own making. If he had not taken the child's place to come and bury the dead . . . But he had had to do it. He was not a coward any more. If only he could live . . . He had not done nearly enough in the forest. He could finish building the school, educate the children, learn how to treat their diseases. He thought he heard noise in the distance and looked up. Was someone coming? Yes, they must be. His heart beat with hope as he peered into the darkness, expecting someone to show up at any moment. They are coming, he thought, and his eyes filled with tears. They will be here any moment now. Yes, yes, I can hear them, he said to himself, convinced that he really did.

17

Venustiano stood at the door with the rifle on his arm and watched the woman. They were leaving behind the few pieces of furniture that he had made for the house when they had married, but even without them they had much more than they could carry on the cow. In a corner of the room the jaguar skin was rolled up and tied. Across the village people moved in and out of their houses hurriedly, but making very little noise. It was already evening and they should be leaving soon. He said, 'Are you done yet?'

The woman shook her head and went on with the packing. The Indian watched her with intense eyes, and the moment she picked up a blackened pot he said, 'Not that. It's too heavy.'

She put the pot down and said, 'It's a shame. Leaving behind so many things . . . '

The Indian said sulkily, 'When this is over, I'll tell them to choose a new leader. There should be many who want to take my place.'

'What do you mean? You are their leader, like your father and your grandfather. That's how it always was.'

'My father,' the Indian said, 'was a foreigner. You think I don't know?'

'Your father was the head of this village.'

'The man you talk about was a drunk who killed himself.'

'He was a good man before the alcohol. I remember — '

'My grandfather was the last good leader of our people. If he were alive today none of this would have happened.'

'It's your duty to look after the people,' the woman said while packing up.

'I've made up my mind. And then they can choose to live in any part of the forest they like — without us.'

'Without us?'

'We'll live on our own. Find some place in the forest.'

'There is nowhere we can go in this forest,' the woman said. 'If the guerrillas look for us, they will find us. It would make no difference whether we lived with the others or not.'

She began to load their things onto the cow as if he were not there. After a while he said, 'That's enough. We have all we need,' but the woman ignored him. He kicked the ground with his naked foot. 'Didn't you hear what I said?'

'I will only listen to my village leader,' the woman said stubbornly.

A distant monkey howled over the chirr-chirr of the crickets and the buzzing of the mosquitoes. After a long pause the Indian said, 'Well, I can't be a village leader without a village.'

'You could be their leader in the town.'

'The town? We aren't going to live in the town. I'll take them there if they want to, and then we three will come back.'

'You have no right to abandon your people.'

'I'm doing it for them. If the guerrillas come after me . . . ' He said sharply, 'Haven't you packed enough?' His voice was tired, it had no anger in it; it was as if he were pleading for mercy. He said, 'We'll have to go soon.'

'It is your right to be head of this village,' the woman said. 'You've proved it.'

'I've proved it?'

'Yes.'

'I've proved the opposite,' the man said and pointed down at the half-deserted village. 'This is happening because of something that I did.'

'It's probably for the best. There will soon be no land left for us here. The squatters will take over.'

'It'll be the same everywhere in a few years.'

'You could get a job in the town.'

'Woman, you speak nonsense.'

She went into the house and came back with the jaguar skin. She unwrapped it and carefully spread it out on the ground without a word. It glowed with a deep amber colour in the light of the hearth fire coming from the house. There was little about it to remind the Indian of the animal that he had killed. He had forgotten the fear he had felt during the hunt too. All that was left was a horrible feeling of emptiness. Only the thought of the boy saved him from utter despair. He said resignedly, 'Go and see where the boy is.'

The woman wrapped up the skin again. She said, 'You killed it.'

'Yes.'

'You risked your life. You hunted it alone.'

'Go now,' he said.

He had to keep watch for the guerrillas. He hitched up the rifle on his shoulder and went towards the forest in the falling dark, his bare feet brushing through the thick undergrowth.

Part Five

18

The light wind carried the distant drone of an engine, and a moment later a white Cessna came into view. Milagros held her hand above her eyes and watched the small plane in the cloudless sky. It was still a novelty to see it coming to land on the narrow strip cleared of trees. She went back to her tent — she did not want to appear to be waiting for it. A large map with several pencil markings on it was spread out on the table: the buildings she had discovered so far. She was measuring the distance between them when the plane touched down. She knew the pilot: a young northerner who flew close to the treetops to impress his passengers. She had never flown in it herself; she preferred to ride the mule to the town, even though it took her three days to get there. She rather liked it — there was hardly any urgency in her visits. Besides, it would not be long before they built a road and she could drive there in a couple of hours.

She went back to work, but could not concentrate. She had been counting the days until the visit and now the plane had come.

Her concern felt petty compared with everything that had happened, but she could not convince herself not to think about it. She drew a few lines with the ruler while listening to the plane taxiing back from the end of the airstrip. The men were going to cut down the trees on a hill nearby tomorrow: it was likely that another building was buried underneath. She wished Moisés were there to see all that — he lived in the town now. The plane engine stopped and she could hear voices.

She opened her notebook and tried to remember the formulas for her calculations: the distance equals the length, times the sines of each angle, divided by . . . She fell silent while she wrote in her notebook as the conversation continued outside. She could not make out the voices clearly — now and then there were little bursts of laughter. It was her workers laughing at something unintelligible one of the visitors had said. She had lost any appetite that she might have for banter perhaps because she rarely went to the town to practise it — she kept to herself in the forest too. Even before what had happened, all her communication with the world had been through letters, which Father Thomas would post in the town for her.

The thought of him made her forget the new arrivals. She often thought about him.

After his death she had finally made the decision to leave the forest, but then she had heard how the Indian and the priest had come across some ruins while fleeing from the guerrillas, and so she had gone to have a look. It had turned out to be more than she had ever expected to find, a whole city hidden away in the forest and the mud. Now she was going to stay here for years to come.

The pencil in her hand hovered over the large map: its tip was as small as the plane had seemed, flying over the vast forest. What was going on outside? The voices grew faint: the workers were probably going to show the visitors the ruins. She was relieved. It was as if she had been hiding from someone who had come very close to finding her, but then had gone away.

Suddenly a shadow fell over the map and a voice said chirpily, 'Hello there.' She looked up, startled, at the man standing at the opening of the tent. He was dressed in a new pair of cargo pants; he was never too keen on expeditions, but he wanted to look the part. 'So there you are,' he said. 'I always wondered how you fitted in.' He looked round, then came cautiously closer and leaned over the map, resting his hands on the table. He gave the map a few cursory glances with an amused smile, like someone looking at a child's drawing. He said, 'Well, you haven't changed at all.' His banal remark went unanswered, and he laughed it off, adding 'Oh, it hasn't been such a long time, I suppose.'

There was a camp bed next to the desk and he took a step towards it, then hesitated and sat down on a crate — perhaps it felt presumptuous to him, for it had been a very long time since the woman and he had lain in the same bed. In another crate artefacts were packed in wood wool — broken pots and figurines and reliefs. He picked one up.

'These are wonderful,' he said. 'Everyone in the museum is very excited, you know.'

'There are some more crates. You should take them on the plane. I can't afford to pay that man to carry them to the town. He charges a fortune.'

'Oh, you shouldn't worry about that. There will be no shortage of funding from now on.'

She finished her surveying calculations and went to a corner of the tent, where she washed her face in a plastic bowl.

'Are you well?' the man said. The woman dried herself and stood at the opening of the tent, looking out. He watched her with curiosity. He said, 'Listen, you don't have to stay. It'd be easy to find someone to take over here. You could still be in charge, of course, and visit whenever you feel like it.'

'I'll stay,' Milagros said. 'I have all the help I need.' She put on her hat. 'Come. I'll show you around.' The afternoon sun was blazing down. She said, 'How long will you be staying?'

The visitor followed her reluctantly. He did not have a hat. 'I am going back the day after tomorrow.'

'Then we shouldn't be wasting any time. It's a very large site. Like I said in the last letter, we have probably searched just one-third of it so far. There are lots more buildings out there.'

She waved her hand in the direction of the forested hills and walked on. The place felt like home to her nowadays — familiar, comfortable, even safe. The guerrillas had not been seen in the area for more than a year. She said, 'Some of the buildings are damaged by explosions. Grenades. The murals and some reliefs are gone. I suppose it could have been worse. At least the roofs haven't collapsed. The walls are forty inches thick.' She climbed the stone steps of the nearest building and waited for the man at the entrance. He breathed heavily and wiped his sweat with the back of his hand. They went inside. She moved slowly in the dark, pausing to shine her torch on the faded paintings on the walls. The man looked at them indifferently, with his hands in his pockets.

'I was worried about you,' he said. 'When I heard about what happened . . . Was it very bad? You should really come back, you know. There's no reason to stay here. What about the rains? I don't know how you can stand this place. I mean, if you are doing all this because . . . ' He looked at the woman, but she said nothing, and he put his glasses on and pretended to study the murals. She kept the torch close to them, and then moved on deeper into the ancient building. Away from the sunlight the temperature had dropped, and her skin prickled with the cool trapped air as she left behind the last traces of daylight and the sounds of the forest. The visitor followed her for a while and then said, 'Thank you. I think I've seen enough.'

Milagros turned back and led the way out of the building and into the intense heat, which made the man groan. He fanned himself with his hand. The only clouds were very far away, high above the mountain range. Down in the plaza the pilot had returned from his walk around the ruins with the workers and climbed into the plane. The visitor and the woman on top of the ancient temple watched the small plane take off, bumping along the grassy airstrip. The man pointed at something in the distance and said, 'What's over there?' and shielded his eyes to see. It was a clearing in the forest, dotted with little black shapes. With his hand held above his eyes, he continued to look at it.

'It's the old village,' the woman said.

'It looks burnt-down.'

'Yes.'

'And the Indians?'

'I wrote to you about it,' Milagros said. 'They moved to the town.' She could not bear to look at it, even though it was nothing but a few dots very far away. The plane flew low over the site, tipped its wings and disappeared noisily in the direction of the town.

'Oh, oh yes,' the visitor said. 'Now I remember. I've been so busy up there. You know how things are always so hectic at that damn museum.' He chuckled. 'Perhaps you're better off here, after all.'

The workers who had watched the plane take off now scattered: it was siesta time. The wide paved plaza stood empty, apart from a few birds pecking about for food. Milagros thought about the Indians living in some slum in the town. She had gone to visit them once, but not again: Moisés had seemed so embarrassed to see her. The governor had tried to convince them to go back, promising

265

them that the army would protect them, but they did not trust him. The visitor said, 'Are you safe here? I could ask the governor for more guards.'

Only Venustiano did not live in the town. She caught a glimpse of him now and then in the forest, always carrying his rifle, probably hunting. She was sure that he saw her too, but he never came close, never even spoke to her from the distance, just slipped out of sight without a sound — like a jaguar. She would have liked to ask him about the boy and the woman. The group of workers sat under a tree eating and laughing. The voices entered her thoughts; it felt like someone cracking jokes at a funeral.

'Do you mind if we go back? I'm very thirsty,' the visitor said, fanning himself. 'This heat is unbearable.' He followed her down the steep steps of the ancient building and they went across the plaza towards the tent, the birds pecking around taking flight ahead of them. She remembered all the letters she had written to him in the months after she had first arrived in the forest. She still had his photo somewhere.

'You know . . . ' the man said uncertainly. They reached the tent and the woman pulled the flap aside and they went in. 'You know, if it weren't for the children . . . '

He let out a sigh of relief: there was no escaping the heat and the humidity, but at least they were out of the sun. Someone had left a bottle of water and two plates of food on the table. He helped himself to the water and began to eat with appetite as sweat trickled down his temples. He looked exactly the way she remembered him from that photo. Where could she have put it? She ought to throw it away.

19

'His Excellency cannot see you now,' the nun said, shutting the heavy door, which she had opened a crack only a moment earlier. She added, as if informing the visitor of a fact that only she was privy to: 'This is the middle of the afternoon.' The young man in the black suit and clerical collar blushed at the shut door a couple of inches from his face and checked his watch again: he was only a few minutes late. While leaving the hotel he had noticed his reflection on the glass door and had quickly returned to his room. Perhaps he should not have done it — but a wrinkled shirt risked making a bad impression. He rang the bell again.

'I have an appointment with His Excellency,' he said with fragile assertiveness when the stern female face reappeared. She said nothing — just shut the door again. A little while later she opened it for a third time, and he silently followed her down a colonnaded cloister to a secluded rose garden. In a corner was a hammock with the bishop, dressed in a white cassock, lying in it. He seemed to be sleeping, but when the nun left, he said in a slow voice, with his eyes shut, 'I had forgotten about our little appointment.'

'I didn't know you were resting, Your Excellency,' the young priest said. 'I could come back later.'

'Stay,' the bishop said, still refusing to open his eyes. 'You like the roses?'

The young man looked round almost with surprise. 'Oh yes, they are quite nice.'

'They are, aren't they? My gardener does a great job. They remind me of that monastery near Rome, the one built on the site of St Benedict's first hermitage.'

'I haven't been . . . '

'It's the place where the saint rolled in the brambles to relieve his carnal longings. When St Francis visited it centuries later he touched the brambles and they were transformed into rose bushes. The rose garden is still there, you know.'

'I'm afraid that I've never been abroad, Your Excellency.'

'Haven't you?' the bishop asked with surprise. A dry cough forced him to open his eyes and he sat up in the hammock, pushed his feet into a pair of sandals and studied his visitor. 'Well, you are very young. You'll get to travel.'

The priest bowed his head. 'If it is God's will.' He thought about all those foreign places he would like to see: New York, London, Madrid and Paris, and Rome of course. It was a dream of his to visit the Holy See and catch a glimpse of His Holiness. How he wished he could get a position there one day.

'I am glad you are here,' the bishop said. He coughed again and rubbed his eyes. At his age it was troublesome to be woken up from a deep sleep. He would tell the sister never to let anyone in again, appointment or no appointment. He ought to have a word with his secretary too. Whoever heard of an appointment at the hour of the siesta? He said, 'In fact I was looking forward to your arrival. Perhaps not to your coming to see me at this unseemly hour, but to your joining the diocese. I've been asking them to send someone for a long time. It's more than a year that the villages in the forest have been without a priest. Ever since that incident.'

'Yes, I was told about it, Your Excellency.'

'A tragedy, a tragedy,' the bishop said, stifling a yawn. He folded his arms over his chest and the eyes under his heavy lids wandered across the rose garden. 'You also know, I guess, that he wasn't one of us,' he said. 'A Jesuit. I don't know why His Holiness bothers with them.'

'I understand he was from England.'

The bishop nodded. 'He was rather distant. All Englishmen are like that, no? It has to do with the weather, you see. The rain. Have you ever been to London — no, of course not, you said that. Well, I haven't, either. To tell you the truth, I never understood him. He had a strange sense of humour too.' He studied the young man in the black suit standing stiffly in front of him and said, 'This is how a priest ought to look. Well done. Don't lose that. Always take good care of yourself. Even if your ministry is . . . ' He hesitated. 'That was another thing with him, you know. He didn't look like a priest. He dressed like a — a . . . a lumberman. You could hardly see his collar under the jacket. As if he were ashamed to be a priest.'

The young man listened attentively: he had great respect for authority. Ever since he was a child he had admired priests and had wanted to become one. It was their calm and dignity and confidence that had impressed him, at an age when he had been tormented by shyness and the fear of sin — any sin. He had supposed that the seminary would have cured him of all that and had been a little disappointed that it had not, not really. He looked down at the flagstones with his hands clasped, while the bishop rocked in his hammock. It was a bad start — to have come at the hour of the siesta and woken an elderly man up like that. He was probably going to think of him as rude and arrogant. But the man he had spoken to on the phone had specifically told him to come. There was a little fountain in the middle of the garden and the sound of the running water was making him thirsty. He thought he had better leave, but he was not sure how to excuse himself. Perhaps the bishop would be offended. He darted a look at him — the old man seemed to have forgotten him, staring down in deep thought. 'Listen,' the bishop said and leaned forward in the hammock, 'I'd understand if you were disappointed.'

'Disappointed, Your Excellency?'

'About the ministry you've been given. You feel cheated, don't you? I don't blame you, my boy. I remember when I first came out of the seminary — all that ambition, those dreams.'

'Oh no, no, not at all, Your Excellency. I am humbled by the great responsibility I am given. I promise to — '

The bishop silenced him with a soothing gesture and a little knowing smile. He thought: they are all the same, those young ones. And so what? That fool of an Englishman was different, and how did that turn out . . . He said, 'It need not be for a long time, if you do your duties well, you know. Just a couple of years in the forest and, assuming nothing unpleasant happens — *quod Deus avertat* — I'll help you get a good parish. Here in the town, for example.'

The young man felt a pang of disappointment: the dream of Rome became even more distant than it was already.

'I was told the village where my predecessor stayed . . . '

'Yes. They burned it down. But there are still some Indians elsewhere in the forest.'

'He,' the priest asked uncertainly, 'he was there a long time, no?'

The bishop smiled. 'Oh, more than a decade. But that was because he wanted to be. Those Englishmen can live all by themselves, they don't mind it. Loneliness means nothing to them. A strange race. I suppose it's a virtue in some ways. That's how they kept an empire going for so long. To tell you the truth, my boy, it suited me too that he didn't want to leave. He had some strange ideas. I'm not sure his faith was very robust. Well, those Jesuits . . . Of course there is always the exception to the rule, and I'm sure there are some good ones too.' He slapped his knees zestfully and said, 'Well, enough about him. It's a sad story. Tell me, you can ride, can't you?'

'Ride? No, Your Excellency.'

'Haven't ridden a mule before?'

'I'm afraid not.'

'Oh. Well, it's easier than riding a horse.'

'No one told me that . . . '

'Never mind, never mind. I'll get someone to show you. You'll learn in no time, you'll see. It's because some of your villages are only accessible by mule, you see. To the rest you can drive quite easily. You can take my jeep. You do drive at least, don't you?'

'Oh yes, yes, Your Excellency. I'm a good driver. I never had a car, but my father — '

'Good then.'

The rose garden glowed in the afternoon sun. The young priest was very thirsty now, but still did not dare ask for water. He wondered what life in the forest would be like. When he had first been told about his appointment he had read everything he could find in the seminary library about it — he was even teaching himself the Indians' language. He had lived all his life in the city, and the idea of travelling alone in that great wilderness terrified him. There was no way out of it: he had taken a vow to do God's will and he would keep it.

The bishop rang a little handbell, and in the still of the afternoon a door creaked and the sound of steps echoed down the cloistered walk. The nun came. The bishop said to his visitor, 'That will be all for now, Father. Thank you for coming to see me. Arrange the details with my capable secretary.'

'Of course, Your Excellency.'

'I am glad to have you with us.' The bishop pulled his feet from his sandals. 'I have a feeling you will do a wonderful job.'

'Thank you.'

'Well then,' the bishop said, and he gathered up his cassock about him and lowered himself into the hammock again. 'Go in peace.'

The young priest bowed and retraced his steps behind the nun down the cloister. Just before going out of the walled garden he glanced back at the bishop lying in the hammock. Suspended in the air above the beds of red roses, his hands folded on his chest and his white cassock glowing in the siesta sun, he seemed to the priest like a happy saint already on his way to heaven.

We do hope that you have enjoyed reading
this large print book.

Did you know that all of our titles
are available for purchase?

We publish a wide range of high quality
large print books including:
**Romances, Mysteries, Classics
General Fiction
Non Fiction and Westerns**

Special interest titles available in
large print are:
**The Little Oxford Dictionary
Music Book
Song Book
Hymn Book
Service Book**

Also available from us courtesy of
Oxford University Press:
**Young Readers' Dictionary
(large print edition)
Young Readers' Thesaurus
(large print edition)**

For further information or a free
brochure, please contact us at:
**Ulverscroft Large Print Books Ltd.,
The Green, Bradgate Road, Anstey,
Leicester, LE7 7FU, England.
Tel:** (00 44) 0116 236 4325
Fax: (00 44) 0116 234 0205

THE CONVENT

Panos Karnezis

The sixteenth-century convent of Our Lady of Mercy stands alone in an uninhabited part of the Spanish sierra, hidden on a hill, among dense pine forest. Its inhabitants are six women, cut off from the world they've chosen to leave behind. This all changes on the day that Mother Superior Maria Ines discovers a suitcase, punctured with air holes, at the entrance to the retreat. She finds the box and its contents are to have consequences beyond her imagining, and that even in her carefully protected sanctuary she is unable to keep the world, or her past, at bay.

LOOK AT ME

Sara Duguid

Lizzy lives with her father Julian and her brother Ig in North London. Two years ago her mother died, leaving a family bereft by her absence and a house still filled with her things. Margaret was lively, beautiful, fun, loving — as far as Lizzy is concerned, she kept the family together. Then, one day, Lizzy finds a letter from a stranger to her father, and discovers he has another child. In an act of outraged defiance, Lizzy invites this new half-sister into her family's world — and, almost immediately, realises her mistake . . .

A VERY SPECIAL YEAR

Thomas Montasser

On a quiet back street in a sleepy town, there sits an old bookshop: an emporium of reading delights. Inside, there sits a most peculiar novel — its ending changes depending on the reader . . . For young Valerie, who has just inherited the shop after the sudden (and very mysterious) disappearance of her Aunt Charlotte, the place amounts to nothing more than a badly-run business, to be whipped into shape before being sold on. But when an enigmatic customer appears and enquires about the novel with no ending, the magic of the place is unlocked . . .

THE GLASGOW COMA SCALE

Neil D. A. Stewart

When Lynne offers money to a homeless man on Glasgow's Sauchiehall Street, she is shocked to recognise him as Angus, her former college art tutor. Lynne once revered him, dreaming of becoming an artist under his tutelage. Now she works in a call centre; and Angus has fallen on even harder times . . . Moved, Lynne insists on inviting him to stay at her flat. But, just as Angus doesn't go out of his way to explain the reasons for his misfortune, Lynne's motivations are not purely altruistic. The more the pair rely upon each other, the more they hate doing so . . .